DATE DUE		

2/22

BOOKS BY WILLIAM F. HALLSTEAD

Ev Kris, Aviation Detective

Dirigible Scout

Sky Carnival

THE MISSILES OF ZAJECAR

WILLIAM F. HALLSTEAD

CHILTON BOOK COMPANY

Philadelphia   New York   London

AUTHOR'S NOTE *The story of the rocket factory near Zajecar and the campaign to destroy it is fiction. But the Nazis actually did develop several surface-to-air missiles late in World War II, although too late to use them effectively.*

Similarly, the Azon guided bomb was used by the USAAF in the closing months of World War II, and later models were employed in Korea.

Details of aircraft described in the story are as accurate as research permits. The 456th Bomb Group (H) and the 747th Squadron were based near Cerignola, Italy, and the base was much as described. However, the events in the story, and the cast of characters, with the exception of General Draza Mihailovic and Reichsmarschall Hermann Goering, are entirely fictitious.

The author apologizes for the sentimental use of the 456th Group and the 747th Squadron designations. They were the group and squadron in which he served as a B-24 radio operator/gunner in 1945.

W. F. H.

THE MISSILES
OF ZAJECAR

ONE

The air was good at twenty-seven thousand feet, smooth under the stubby wings of Major Erwin Buckler's shark-gray Focke–Wulf 190D, and crystal clear. The somber mountains of eastern Serbia, the Transylvanian Alps, rolled brokenly to the horizon. Buckler believed he could even have seen Belgrade, the capital of Yugoslavia, eighty miles to the northwest were it not for the shoulders of the Transylvanian cliffs crouching gunmetal blue along the north.

Buckler hated these mountains. They were mist-ridden and cold in the mornings, forbidding when the sun sank beyond them to the Adriatic Sea two hundred miles west. Those brooding Alps at this forsaken juncture of Yugoslavia, Rumania, and Hungary, were a far cry from the emerald fields of his beloved Saxony in the German homeland. They were evil. They invited wild imaginings. That, after all, was why The Project was located here.

1

He could not help but think of the project in capital letters. Far below him, on Rtanj Mountain, near Zajecar, Yugoslavia, some of the best scientific minds in the Reich worked feverishly, fighting, with their slide rules and testing gauges, a race with the calendar. The hour was late in this spring of 1944. But the direction of the war would yet turn, and Germany's decisive weapon against the Allies would come out of this remote fastness in the Balkans.

It would come, that is, if Major Buckler and the thirty yellow-nosed fighter planes of his command could always do as well against the American bombers as they had this morning.

Buckler smiled beneath his oxygen mask. Kommando Boelcke, the special squadron assigned to defend The Project, and under his personal command, had performed faultlessly. Of the twelve fat B-24 bombers that had lumbered into his defense area some twenty minutes ago, five had been blown from the air by the 20mm cannon of his Focke-Wulfs. Two more had lost altitude and disappeared westward in long flat glides, trailing pencil lines of black smoke across the china-blue sky. That had accounted for seven. The remaining bombers had huddled together, put their heads down like obstinate buffaloes, and plunged through the Focke-Wulfs to loose their bombs on the rail junction near Zajecar.

Pulling off to give Zajecar's few anti-aircraft guns their minutes of futile glory, the pilots of Kommando Boelcke were somewhat confused by the fact that only four of the five remaining B-24's banked away from their target and scurried westward toward the base in Italy, from which they had come. The victory was considerable, but Buckler wanted it tied in a neat package. His squadron had, on the face of it, shot down eight bombers and had obviously

2

forced the Americans to drop their bombs far short of their primary target. Still, he could account for only seven of the eight downed planes: five on the way in and the two that had glided westward, to be found, no doubt, piled up somewhere in southern Serbia by ground parties before darkness fell. The eighth bomber had simply disappeared. That bothered Major Buckler.

He sent his pilots back to their pebbly field at the base of Rtanj Mountain for fresh ammunition and fuel. He, too, needed fuel, but with enough gasoline to keep his engine roaring a few more minutes, he wanted to tie up this one loose end.

He circled slowly, his eyes darting along the barren creases where silver threads cut swiftly toward a distant river valley. Nothing. Not a single wisp of smoke to mark the end of the eighth B-24.

Major Buckler pursed his lips thoughtfully. He was an exceptionally handsome man, blond, with deep-water cobalt eyes, and his good looks had helped him considerably in the attainment of his rank. The Home Front needed photogenic heroes. Major wasn't a bad achievement for a pilot barely twenty-three years old. The photographs in the Berlin papers of the blond, trim, smiling Leutnant Erwin Buckler dismounting his Messerschmitt after a sweep across the English Channel had caught the eye of the Luftwaffe's high command. His progress was watched carefully. After thirty victories, he was given promotions in quick succession and his own squadron along the Atlantic Wall.

Then Buckler's squadron, named for publicity reasons the Kommando Boelcke after the World War I ace, had been pulled out of France. The Atlantic Wall was, after all, impregnable with or without them, and a crack fighter unit was urgently needed to defend The Project that was now underway in the remote mountains of Yugoslavia. Assigned the highest priority status, Kommando Boelcke was supplied with brand-new Focke-Wulf 190D's—the first off the assembly line—and sent to Rtanj Mountain.

Fifteen minutes ago, Buckler had shot down his fifty-first plane. He despised the B-24's. They were unpretty, their long tapering wings worthy of a better design than that provided by their fat, chunky fuselage and ugly twin rudders. Their wing, Buckler had learned from intelligence reports, was a special airfoil, something called a "Davis section," which gave the big four-engined plane unexpected speed and allowed it to carry a heavier load than the more pleasing-to-the-eye B-17.

The Americans had named the B-17 "Flying Fortress," and the name was almost accurate—the B-17 was tough as a mastiff. The B-24 was called the "Liberator," a vague sort of a name for a bomber, Buckler thought, but more interesting to him than her name was the B-24's curious vulnerability. The B-24 flew higher, faster, and carried more load than the B-17. But she had a magnificent flaw. Hit her square amidships—right in the shoulder blades between the wing roots where all the fuel cross-feed lines were located—and she became a beautiful fireball.

Buckler's eyes roamed along the winding stream that was the Crna River skirting Rtanj Mountain. Far below, the tiny gray crosses that were his squadron circled their rugged little airstrip and settled in for refueling, rearming, and quick repairs of any stray bullet holes the B-24 gunners had chanced to score. He smiled tightly. Bomber gunners were more-or-less ineffective, except as psychological hazards. His pilots knew that, and he suspected that the American gunners knew it, too. That, he had heard, was the reason they used tracers every fourth round: simply to inform the attacking pilot that he was being shot at.

A tiny glint of reflected sunlight caught his eye. The windshield of a truck? But there was no road along that shadowed mountainside. He thrust down the nose of his Focke-Wulf and peeled away six thousand feet before he made out the dusky outline of the camouflaged B-24 limping westward among the mountains. A moment later, he was close enough to see that one of its engines was out of action, its propeller silhouetted against the rock-strewn wastes a thousand feet below.

Erwin Buckler fingered the electric cannon switch. This would be number fifty-two. A full deck, the newspapers might call it.

First Lieutenant Jesse C. ("Never-mind-what-the-C-stands-for"—it stood for Crittenden) Stafford was in the throes of such desperation as he had never dreamed possible. And the day had started off so routinely back at the base near Foggia, Italy. "A milk run," Ed Tanner, the intelligence briefing officer, had called it. "So routine, you guys shouldn't even get credit toward your thirty-five. The target is the rail junction at Zajecar in eastern Yugoslavia. Lot of traffic going through there recently, probably supplies for the Russian front. You can expect a few anti-aircraft guns around the target. Not much of it. More of an exercise for the home guard they've managed to recruit among the kids and old men. We figure they've got a few beat-up 88's and maybe some old Rumanian-made guns."

"Any fighters?" one of the pilots had asked.

"Not unless somebody's deserting from the Russian front." And they had all laughed. But the sky suddenly full of brand new FW 190 fighters made that laugh seem hollow now. For nearly five minutes, the air over the Morava River was torn by destruction. Hennessey's bunch went down under the Focke-Wulfs' guns. Ed Moleski blew up just off

5

Stafford's left wing. Moleski had been there like glue, for hours. Then, in an eye's single wink, Moleski's B-24 had bloomed like a great orange rose, and the sky had a hole in it where a plane had been.

Jesse's tail gunner called two more down: Adams curving away at the end of a boiling smoke rope and Mike Forsythe plunging behind a hill with his left wing wrapped back over the fuselage, engines and all.

It was hideous. Then it was over. The German fighters pulled away—out of fuel or ammunition or both. Jesse's crew had been too busy to see the other three bombers go down. But, in addition to Jesse's ship, only four others came out the other side of the Focke-Wulf meatgrinder, regrouped around him, and bore down on the rail yard. At that point, the mission took on the routine nature that had been predicted. The flak meant nothing, bursting a thousand feet too low and to the right. The bombs burst along the converging tracks, and the B-24's banked steeply south to make their homeward run.

"Number Three's running rough as cobblestones," Lieutenant Stavros Kavalla, Jesse's co-pilot, said suddenly.

Jesse's green-brown eyes swept the engine instruments. He had one choice. "Feather it." The propeller ran down and stopped, its blades turning into the wind. Radioman Staff Sergeant Charley Charles—"Si-Si to my friends" —peered through his little plastic bubble window and clearly read the words "Hamilton Standard" on the dead prop. That was upsetting.

But not nearly as upsetting as the fact that the other four B-24's had already pulled away, per standing order, and left their crippled comrade to the wolves.

Jesse felt no anger. This was a no-holds-barred war, and you didn't hang around risking nine-man crews to escort a buddy who probably wouldn't make it back anyway.

He thumbed his throat mike button. "Stafford to crew. We're on our own. Keep sharp, now. We're still going home."

He hoped. The Focke-Wulfs seemed to have evaporated, but if they hadn't, he figured their eyes were on the surviving flight of four Libs now swinging southward. He throttled back slightly and let the heavy bomber sink. Stav's eyes questioned him above his oxygen mask, and Jesse made a swooping motion with his gloved right hand. They were going to hedgehop home. Stav shrugged, and Jesse knew what his words would be if this were a routine ride without intercom discipline. "Whatever you say, Jess. You're driving the bus."

Far east of Zajecar, Jesse found what he wanted: a deep valley that wound back westward into a network of passes and cols that would see them clear of the fighter area. Beyond that, a lone B-24 rushing low over southern Yugoslavia shouldn't have too much trouble getting past poorly-organized ground defenses. And if they went down, the Partisans or Chetniks fighting with the Allies were active through most of the area.

The Liberator sank below mountain-top level, and the howl of its three good engines shook pebbles loose on the steep mountainsides. The oxygen masks came off. They were headed toward safety, and with luck, would all eat supper in a Foggia restaurant. My treat, too, Jesse vowed silently.

Then, like the sand in an hourglass that had been sinking lower all the time, luck ran out.

"Fighter six o'clock high." That would be Sergeant Terrible Terry Cochran crouched in his Emerson tail turret. He'd earned his nickname back in Overseas Training at

7

Chatham Field, Savannah, when his camera guns had "brought down" not only the darting P-63 target plane, but the B-24 behind him as well. "It was only a camera," he'd pointed out repeatedly with good Irish humor, but the nickname stuck. It wasn't only a camera now. He pulled the charging handles of his twin fifties.

"Focke-Wulf," said Sergeant Morry Flax in his Martin upper turret. Jesse heard the turret assembly grind as Morry brought his guns to bear.

"I'll fly," Jesse said. "You fight." This was the rotten part of piloting a bomber. You sat here and you took it. For a fleeting moment he envied the gunners. At least they had a chance to shoot back. But that was no picnic, either. If the pilot's compartment got it, good night, Irene, for everybody.

Jesse stole a look over his right shoulder. Si-Si's rear end was fast disappearing aft through the empty bomb bay as he rushed to join Staff Sergeant Frank "Hunky" Molnar, the flight engineer, in the waist. During combat, each of the staff sergeants manned a waist window gun.

Just forward, Jesse made out the helmeted top of Sergeant Hiram Sanderson's head in the nose turret. Sandy had swung his turret sharply sideways and was trying to screw his head around far enough to get a look at what was coming.

In the Sperry ball turret beneath the long belly, Sergeant Nick Pastore muttered to himself, taking care not to depress his mike button. "Fine-fine-fine. First guy to hit the ground is me. Only guns can't reach him are mine." That was a very tough break for Stafford's crew, because in contrast to the general marksmanship of aerial gunners, Nick Pastore was something of a dead-eye.

8

Another crew member feeling sorry for himself at this moment was Navigator-Bombardier Howard Ennis, known as "Skinny." A flight officer—"that's limbo between master sergeant and shavetail, but they pay me anyway"—Skinny looked down at his right hand which had leaped by reflex to the butt of his forty-five automatic. He laughed bitterly. The forty-five was loaded with birdshot, the customary ammunition for overwater flights. Seagulls could make good eating for a man in a raft. Maybe some day they'll give bombagators a nail to bite on, he thought ruefully.

The Focke-Wulf grew larger in Terrible Cochran's glowing gunsight reticle. He depressed the twin triggers, and the sharp pounding ran the length of the ship. Four guns on the Focke-Wulf winked briefly. The basketful of cannon shells shrieked across the nose of the B-24, almost a complete miss. But not quite. A shell tore into the nose turret and exploded flatly above the engines' thunder. A biting smell of cordite drifted into the flight deck, and, instantly, Skinny Ennis was on the intercom. "Got Sandy! In the leg. An artery, I think."

"Can you stop it?" Jesse fought to keep his voice level. "Make a tourniquet with his belt, Skinny." Jesse had never had a wounded man before—not in twenty-three missions. "Si-Si, get up here!" The radioman on heavy bombers was responsible for first aid. "Where'd that fighter get to, somebody? Come on, report, report."

"Behind that hill to our left," Morry cut in from his view atop the plane. "Swinging around for another—there he is, coming in level at six o'clock about five miles behind us." The German fighter was low on the broken horizon, a little winged dot growing fast.

"He's good," Stav said, searching Jesse's eyes.

9

"I'll say he's good. One burst, one hit."

Skinny was on the intercom again, his voice high and thin. "Sandy's got to get help, Jess. He's still bleeding."

"What about the tourniquet?"

"We're doing all we can—but he's not going to make it without a hospital."

"Don't tell *him* that!"

"His headset's off."

"Well, there sure isn't any hospital around here."

"How about a morgue," Cochran put in. "I'd say we all have two minutes. He's closing in right now."

"One burst," Nick Pastore pleaded. "One burst. I'll guarantee ya—"

An idea flared in Jesse's mind. No, he wouldn't do it. Couldn't.

"We've got the bleeding under control for the moment," Skinny's voice broke in. "A nice soft landing and a hospital could save this guy."

The fighter barreled past, its foreign howl audible above the familiar Pratt & Whitneys. In its wake, chunks of elevator and left rudder flew into the slipstream and fluttered away. The thumping of the upper turret stopped. "He's playing with us," Morry Flax said bitterly. "He's coming around again."

Jesse decided to put his conscience in storage for a better day. "All right, everybody. Do exactly as I tell you."

To Erwin Buckler's amazement, the lumbering B-24 suddenly soared up from the valley and put a thousand feet of clear air beneath its belly. It was suicide. He had them before, but now he could really maneuver. Toying with the big bomber wasn't really unsporting, he felt. After all, he

10

could have blown it out of the air on his first pass. This way, he'd given it a few more minutes of life.

The Focke-Wulf banked steeply and slid toward the tail of the Liberator in a traditional pursuit curve. Buckler liked more flashy attacks, but it was a good idea not to forget anything in the instruction book.

His gunsight caught the Liberator; held it. This would be the last pass. His fuel was getting too low. He began to depress the cannon switch—then lifted his finger in astonishment.

The bomber was lowering its wheels.

The surrender signal! He'd heard of this, but he had never seen it. An occasional enemy bomber pilot, with all hope gone and certain death inches away, was known to have let down his wheels and allowed his plane to be shepherded to the nearest German base.

What a prize! And what newspaper copy. Buckler's sand-colored eyebrows rose in eager contemplation. He pulled up, then circled the B-24 warily. It continued westward, but he could see white faces at the waist windows staring at him. The bomber's guns were silent, all pointing skyward except those of the bottom turret, which pointed straight down. The squadron markings were clearly visible, a white thunderbolt running diagonally across the scarlet rudders with the black numerals "401" in the upper portion.

Buckler was elated. He slid closer, then held steady a hundred yards from the bomber's left side. He pulled even with the pilot and pointed northeastward. The left wing of the olive-colored B-24—huge at this distance—began to lift in the required right turn.

Something was wrong. In an instant, the ball turret guns had flipped upwards. As the bomber swung away in a tight bank, the tail turret lined up on him. In the left waist win-

11

dow, only one face remained. It crouched over the gun mounted on the sill.

A trick! Furious, Buckler slammed his throttle home and yanked back the control column. Five sprays of fifty-caliber slugs converged on him. His disdain of bomber gunners was shattered in the slivered plexiglas of the cockpit canopy.

Smoke boiled from Buckler's engine cowling, closing his throat. Now his ship fell off and screeched toward the rocks. Buckler fought into a semi-controlled glide, but the engine clanked and died, leaving behind a shrill whistle of slipstream. An oily streak of flame licked back to sear his cheeks. High above him, the B-24 banked west again, its wheels folding neatly into the wing wells.

The oil fire was brighter now, a frightening glow through the choking smoke. He was too low to eject. Off to the left, a crag whisked past. He could make out the individual rocks.

Buckler booted the fighter into a steep sideslip— dangerous in a low-winged plane with surfaces so stubby— but there was no other way to see ahead. The maneuver swept the flames away for a moment. He spotted a gravelly stream-bed a half-mile ahead.

He came in fast and flat. The long tail eased down. Flying speed faded. The fighter's armored belly screeched across the rubbly creek-bottom. Dual fans of spray exploded from the little creek. The left wing dropped, and a huge boulder tore away its outboard section.

The battered Focke-Wulf shuddered to a stop, its long fuselage broken and its engine flaming brightly. Buckler fought free of the clutching safety straps. Fire washed over him in a searing dragon's roar. He rolled over the edge of the cockpit and stumbled toward the deepest water, ripping off his melting goggles. The icy wetness hissed into his

12

smoldering collar, and he plunged his head under the swiftly flowing surface. The remaining cannon shells in his wing guns exploded above him with flat *pungs,* then only crackling flames broke the silence.

The awful searing resumed the instant he came up for air, and he forced himself to crawl on numbed hands and knees up the stream bank. As he collapsed, a solid shred of clarity reached through the delirium of pain. A number.

He pinned all the concentration he had left onto that number. And when the three-man German military police patrol put him on a stretcher twenty minutes later, he found consciousness long enough to gasp through clenched teeth, *"Vier-Null-Eins."* 401.

TWO

The engines of the last B-24 to limp home died in a flurry of hot clanking. Across the flat plain southwest of Foggia, through the almond orchard where new green was beginning to shade the crew members' tents from the Italian sun, a silence settled. It was the stunned hush that falls over an air base when news of a disaster has reached even the sweating cooks in the mess halls. It was the wordless agony of seven maintenance crew chiefs learning that their planes and their crews were not coming back. It was the tight-lipped frustration of the officer in charge of aircraft supply, trying to forget sixty-three faces by concentrating on the question of where in all of Southern Italy he could get his hands quickly on seven replacement B-24's and seven crews.

But in the debriefing building, a long frame shed near the maintenance hangar, silence was not in order. The 456th

Group's air intelligence staff moved from crew to weary crew, their pencils poised over their clipboards, gathering the pieces of information that they would try to assemble into a picture of what had happened on the mission. The 747th Squadron's Captain Edgar Tanner was head of the air intelligence detachment. Like all of his men, he was outwardly unemotional and inwardly unrelenting. He knew that Jesse Stafford's crew were bone-tired, shaken by what they had been through, and far more stunned than himself by the loss of so many men. They had, after all, seen it happen.

But Captain Tanner's job was to get information, get it while it was fresh. He ran his fingers through his thin dark hair and tapped the pencil point on the earpiece of his steel-rimmed glasses. His beefy boxer's face registered a series of subtle changes: surprise, then doubt, then puzzlement.

"Focke-Wulf 190D's you said. A brand-new model being used in that God-forsaken area? That's hard to believe."

"Well, believe it or not, sir," Terrible Cochran said wearily, "that's what they were."

"If Cochran says so," said Jesse Stafford, "that's it. There isn't a plane built that he can't identify inside of five seconds."

"You people were dead wrong about fighter defense today," said Stav Kavalla, with obvious bitterness.

Tanner looked at him coldly, decided it was not a challenge but a barbed statement of fact, and said, "With the help of all of you, we're trying to find out exactly why." He turned to Jesse. "You don't think those FW's could have been on some sort of reassignment trip to or from the Russian front? Maybe they just stumbled across your flight and decided to freelance."

Jesse shook his bear-like crewcut head slowly. Tanner

15

could see that all two hundred pounds of him was on the ragged edge. "That last guy hung with us like he had all the fuel and ammo in Germany. He had to be based somewhere around there."

"Mmm." Tanner sounded as though he had lost interest in that particular point. But his mind was racing. Stafford's comment could be all-important. He felt an almost overpowering urge to race for the target summary map in his office. But the debriefing of this crew was not yet over. There was another matter to kill.

"You said that you and Sergeant Pastore managed to shoot down the fighter that attacked your plane?" The question was addressed to Si-Si Charles.

"And Terrible—Sergeant Cochran, Sir. All three of us hit him at once from close range."

"How close?"

"About a hundred yards—" Si-Si stopped and flicked a glance at Jesse.

"A hundred yards?" Tanner persisted, catching the flicker of Si-Si's eyes. "A mere three hundred feet? This fighter got that close without blowing you out of the air? You realize that model carries four cannon?"

The way the entire crew stared at the plank table top struck Tanner as fascinating. He itched to probe further, but he always recognized the point at which combat crews had reached their limit. From here on, they would grow irritated and defensive. He stood up.

"All right, gentlemen. I thank you for your help. That'll be all."

There are two problems here, thought Tanner as he went through the stack of intelligence questionnaires in his office. Beyond the open window, he heard the familiar sounds of the 456th Bombardment Group pulling itself together after

16

a bad day. The 745th and the 746th squadrons had been part of a heavy combined strike against southern Austria. Two bombers had been lost between them. His own 747th had drawn the mission against Zajecar that had turned into a nightmare. Now the metallic sounds of repair reached him from the nearby hangar and the hardstands where the ground crews were back at their endless task of riveting, welding, and performing other noisy activities.

Yes, there were two problems. He pulled a clean sheet of paper from his desk drawer, drew a line down the center, and headed the columns "Item 1" and "Item 2."

Unconsciously he muttered to himself as he scratched words in the first column. "Apparently a top-notch Focke-Wulf unit . . . brand-new planes. . . . Zajecar! That's the end of the world! . . . Wait a minute . . . where's that report we got last week . . ."

He leafed through a stack of onionskin in a manila folder stamped "CONFIDENTIAL."

Yeah, this is it. "Air Force liaison with Mihailovic near Belgrade reports unusual amount of supplies going toward Zajecar. Unmarked sealed boxcars . . . only specific observation was of boxcar derailed by Chetniks. Alcohol in metal drums."

Tanner rubbed his chin thoughtfully. Alcohol? How did that get by him when he'd read this last week? That's the trouble with a job like this: never enough time to do it—makes you sloppy sometimes. He grabbed his telephone.

"Get me Air Intelligence at Wing, please. Major Kelleher." There was a pause filled with clicking and assorted buzzes. This line was supposed to be on code scrambler, but he decided to play it safe.

"Kelleher? Tanner. 456th. Better request a visual of area T-seven. That's right, Fred, on my say-so."

Kelleher clicked off, and now the wheels were in motion. From Wing Headquarters in Foggia, a coded message would go to joint British-American OSS operations control in southwestern Italy. Within hours, a few key words inserted into a regular Serbian-language propaganda broadcast to Yugoslavia would tell the headquarters of Draza Mihailovic that the United States Army Air Force needed information from the area of Zajecar. It was easy enough to request this kind of thing, Tanner reflected. Lord knew what would happen at the other end.

He stared briefly across the airfield to the black-topped perimeter, where a hopelessly battered engine was being lowered by block, tackle, and muscle from flak-torn nacelle. The call to Wing had temporarily taken care of Problem One. What about Problem Two?

Something was wrong with Stafford's crew. Anyone could see that. They had absolutely clammed up when he asked for details on their kill. Odd. Usually, when a crew had gotten a fighter, you couldn't hold them down. But Stafford's men had given their pilot a quick look and that was the end of it.

Tanner took off the glasses that had kept him out of the air and rubbed the bridge of his nose with thumb and forefinger. This was some job for an ex-certified public accountant. Problem Two, he was afraid, would have to remain Stafford's own for the time being. Unless it endangered the crew's combat effectiveness, Tanner did not wish to get into what appeared to be a private situation.

He shouted for Corporal Olshinsky in the outer office. Maybe a cup of Olshinsky's fierce coffee would get his mind off Stafford's crew and onto something he could understand.

Two hundred yards away in their six-man tent in the almond grove, Jesse Stafford's crew were finding that no

18

amount of Si-Si's over-boiled coffee would drown the thing they were trying to avoid. Finally Terrible put it in words that hung in the smoky tent.

"What we're all wondering is this, isn't it: how sporting is it to shoot down a guy who thinks you're surrendering?"

After a long silence, Nick said, "That about sums it up, if 'sporting' is the word."

"Ask Sandy," Hunky Molnar said, his jaw bones rippling aggressively. "You'll find him resting comfortably in the hospital at Wing Headquarters. Alive."

"But suppose we hadn't had a wounded man aboard," said Morry Flax. The situation intrigued him. At twenty-eight, he was the old man of the crew, four years older than Stafford himself. Morry was thin and slightly stooped, bearing a certain resemblance to a farmer, though he had never been closer to a farm than the grocery store he'd managed for his uncle in Boston. A store was a good place to study people, Morry had found, and he'd made the most of the opportunity. The Air Force was a good place for that, too. "Just suppose nobody had been wounded, what then?"

Si-Si looked up from his cot. "I don't know what Jesse would have done in that case, and I don't think he does, either." His narrow face was serious as he twitched back a swatch of brown hair from his forehead.

"Are you all crazy?" Nick suddenly exploded, his heavy black brows meeting in a frown. "The kraut was going to do us, and we did him instead. That's all there is to it."

"Maybe that's the way you live longer in Philadelphia," Terrible said acidly.

Nick eyed him. "No, that's the way you live longer in a war."

Si-Si stared at the floor. "There wasn't any fun in it."

Hunky Molnar's face registered shock. *"Fun!"*

"No, no. That's not the word I mean. You know. Thrill, maybe. That's what I expected. Some kind of thrill. Maybe he was too close. I could see him looking at us."

"Just shut up," Nick snapped, "all of you! We shot down a kraut who was hoping to shoot us down. That's it. End of report. Now shut up."

"Yeah, forget it," Hunky urged. "It's chow time."

Si-Si stood up and reached for his mess kit. "You can forget it, Hunky. You were at the other window. You couldn't even see it. Nick, Terrible, and I shot him down. I wonder if *we* can forget it."

In the officers' tent area at the other end of the almond grove, Stav Kavalla checked his watch. "Have you seen Jesse?" he asked Skinny Ennis. "He hasn't come back since debriefing and that was an hour ago."

"Yeah, I saw him. He was walking up and down the road along the hard-stand line. Back and forth. I asked him to come back for coffee, but he acted like he didn't know I was there."

Stav's pleasant dark face grew somber. "You mean he didn't even answer?"

"Not a nod. What do you make of it, Stav?"

The stocky little co-pilot didn't answer. After several silent minutes that put Skinny completely on edge, he said, "You know what's the matter with air crews? They're made out of guys who are specially selected because they think. We think, Skinny. And we have too much time between these rotten missions to do it."

"You want to come with me to get Jesse?"

"No, let him work it out. He's no different than the rest of us."

"I don't know about that, Stav. You didn't see his face."

THREE

The general looked far older than his years. The thick, combed-back black hair, heavy over his prominent ears, did not hide the fatigue in the narrow eyes behind his thin-rimmed glasses. There was a touch of gray over the high temples, and there was iron-gray in the full beard that flowed luxuriously from ear to ear and to the open collar of the heavy brown Royal Yugoslav Army tunic. He kept its eight large buttons shining, although the uniform was hopelessly rumpled and stained. The glittering buttons were unconscious symbols of his once unshakable belief that the war would end in victory and that the Royal Family once again would rule his shattered country.

But now, in this year of 1944, the general was past that belief, nearing the end of hope. He was certain of only one thing: the Germans were faced with defeat. Beyond that,

21

who could say for sure what would happen to his beloved Yugoslavia?

It was a pity that the country was not composed entirely of Serbs. Under his leadership, these tough eastern Yugoslavs had been the first to take up arms against the invading Nazis. The Germans had learned to dread his Chetniks. For every German soldier killed by the French resistance, the Germans shot perhaps six Frenchmen, but for each Nazi soldier waylaid by the Chetniks, a full one hundred Serbs fell before German machine guns.

The general would never admit it to the handful of old royalists who had followed him to this mountain hideout southwest of Belgrade, but he knew that his influence in Yugoslavia's future was nearing its end. The Germans, the Hungarians, the Italians, the Bulgarians—all would be swept from Yugoslavia by an Allied victory. But not that man, Broz. No, Josip Broz—the one they called Tito—was the man to reckon with. Close-shaven, cold-eyed, unsmiling, Broz was as detestable to the general as the tall, big-helmeted Nazis themselves. He was a *communista,* no doubt under the direction of the Comintern. "His razor is German," someone had once said, "his soap is Czech, his shirt is from Russia. Stay away from that one." But Josip Broz had outsmarted the royalist Chetniks and the fanatic Croatian Ustasha under that madman, Ante Pavelic. All but Pavelic's followers fought the Nazis, and all fought each other. But Tito and his people talked about a wonderful, if vague, future where every man would have a share of the victory—whatever that meant. Against this, the Chetniks offered a return to the monarchy, a realistic promise, but one which carried mixed memories. And Pavelic's Ustasha? They promised an iron fist.

These thoughts all rushed through General Draza Mi-

22

hailovic's mind as he struggled exhaustedly to bring his attention back to the words of his interpreter, a small black-haired girl who looked too delicate for her badly fitting brown uniform.

". . . Major Palanka's request, General Mihailovic," she repeated to him with a look of concern.

They know I am slipping, the general admitted to himself. All these months of running, striking and running, the only way I have left to fight . . . *"Da.* Yes," he said. "Would you ask him to repeat it?"

The girl said patiently, "The major has received a request from OSS for a report on Zajecar, general. We have already reported much railroad traffic to that area from the northwest. They do not believe it is going on to the Russian front."

Mihailovic's eyes shifted to Major Palanka, standing stiffly in the musty goatherd's cabin that served as their headquarters. Palanka, despite his Serbian name, was as American as President Roosevelt. He had dropped out of the dark sky in a black parachute one night ten months ago and had served with the general day and night ever since. A Chicagoan born of naturalized Serbian parents, Palanka had turned guerrilla fighter overnight, and Mihailovic was proud of him. But nevertheless, he lacked the true spirit. He was first an American major, only second a guerrilla. He played the game well, but it was just that—a game. For the rest of them, serving here in the Serbian wilds was their life. For Palanka it was only a job.

Mihailovic pulled his gaze back to the girl. "It is important, this business around Zajecar?"

She put the question to Palanka, and he answered with an emphasis so strong that the force of it came straight through the language barrier.

"He says," she translated, "that it is possible the end of the war depends on the information we are able to send to his people."

An exaggeration, of course. But the major's eyes met the general's without wavering. Perhaps it was true, thought the general. Perhaps this was his final chance to be useful in a once-great cause that had disintegrated into so many scattered causes that he no longer knew where his own course lay.

He folded his arms and sat stiffly behind the wide wooden table for a long moment.

"Lazar," he said at last, the name fairly exploding the tense silence. "He is the man for this one."

The major saluted, about-faced, and strode from the hut's gloom into the bright mountain sunshine. The girl caught up with him, and they stood together, looking far across the beautiful silent valley.

"What do you think, major?" she said in her musical English. "The general is not well, is he?"

"He's tired," Palanka answered, "we all are, but he most of all. I'm tired of ten months of fighting, but he is tired of a thousand years of it."

"You know our history."

"And I'm afraid of what's happening to you now. Of course, I won't be here for whatever the Allied victory may bring you. But General Mihailovic will."

Fourteen hours later, as dawn sent bright spears of sunlight deep into the gloomy mountain passes just east of the town of Paracin, Yugoslavia, a solitary man pedaled his rusty bicycle relentlessly southward. He was not an impressive figure in his flapping blue jacket and baggy gray trousers. A moth-eaten rucksack was slung over his shoulder, and a faded brown hat perched casually above his high forehead. A few strands of thin hair dangled over his eyes. The black moustache on his long upper lip was bunched like a paint brush beneath his blade-like nose. This lone bicyclist was a country man dressed in what was left of his best suit in this poor section of Serbia. Or so he appeared. But the carelessly dressed cyclist was Lazar.

He had simply appeared on the deserted hard-packed gravel road at dawn, emerging unobserved from a mountain path. That hadn't been difficult. The road eastward from Paracin to Zajecar was lightly travelled, he had heard, and checked only by an occasional patrol. The only real danger would come when he tried to slip past the new German fighter base near Rtanj Mountain, thirty-two kilometers away. A few kilometers beyond the airfield lay three tiny settlements, then the Zajecar railhead.

Lazar hunched over the handlebars and set a fast steady pace through the chilly morning. His bicycle was much like himself—it was seedy-looking and seemingly tired, but, like his own, its appearance was a careful deception. It was in top condition.

And Lazar? He was no shambling peasant at all, but a shrewd Chetnik with an uncanny ability to turn any situation to his own advantage. He walked as though he'd been born behind a plow, but before the war he had been a professor of languages at the University of Belgrade. In addition to his native Serbian, he spoke fluent German, English, and French. He had chosen as his code name that of the legendary Serbian folk hero, Czar Lazar. No one remembered his real name now, and he fully expected to die simply as "Lazar," a hard-working unglamorous man who loved his

25

country. If anyone had called him a hero, he would have laughed in his peculiar tight-mouthed way. Heroes, Lazar believed, could not possibly feel the cold fear he felt through every assignment. No one could have convinced him that true heroes are those who face peril in spite of fear.

Lazar's lean legs drove him closer to the bluish crag that towered beyond the scattered trees along the roadway. Rtanj Mountain. He pumped heavily up a long rise and paused briefly at its crest. Ahead, the road curved along the skirt of the mountain, and thirty meters below ran the ice-blue ribbon of the Crna River. A mile from the Crna, the rolling countryside flattened into a broad valley. The valley of the hawks. There they lurked, their gray wings catching the mid-morning sun. Tiny from here, the German fighters appeared as children's toys, carefully placed on a gray-green rug, with the chalky towers of an ancient monastery hunching above them on the far side of the valley.

But the airfield was not Lazar's concern. Getting past it was. He pushed off and pedaled toward the mountain, the tightly-inflated tires popping an occasional pebble into the stiff grass on the side of the road.

Lazar heard the engine long before he saw the motor-cycle and its bounding sidecar rounding the mountain's edge ahead of him. Because he could be easily observed from the airfield by anyone with field glasses, he knew there was more danger in hiding from the motorcycle patrol than in meeting it. The helmets of the driver, and of the trooper behind a light machine gun in the sidecar, shone in the distance. Military police, Lazar determined. Probably a routine patrol for airfield security.

The cycle and sidecar grew larger and noisier, veered

26

into the middle of the road in front of him, and stopped with the machine gun's slim barrel dead on him.

The driver shut off his engine and swung from his seat, tucking his black gloves under his belt. He was a tall non-commissioned officer, scowling under his pot-like helmet, his gray uniform well-pressed. Wehrmacht, Lazar noted— Regular army, thank God. Not SS.

"Pass." The officer held out a hand for Lazar's papers and leafed arrogantly through the forged documents. *"Wohin gehen Sie?"*

Lazar looked at him blankly. *"Ich verstehe—uh—nicht.* I do not understand."

There was nothing to be gained by revealing his knowledge of German.

The soldier grimaced. *"Gde?* Where? Where do you travel?" he asked in halting Serbian, curling the corner of his mouth in obvious distaste at being forced to strike out into a language he wasn't sure of.

"I dem u Lubnica," said Lazar. "I'm going to Lubnica. My sister is very ill. I have permission from the occupation office in Paracin to see her."

The German held up a hand, palm out. *"Govorite sporije.* Speak more slowly. Who is sick?"

"My sister. Nada Kavpac. In Lubnica. *Verstehe? Verstehe?"*

"Yes, yes. I understand, old bumpkin. Don't shout at me." The young German's Serbian wasn't as bad as he had led Lazar to believe, and Lazar took that as a silent warning. He stared at his dusty shoes, letting the soldier carry the conversation.

"Your sister is in Lubnica, you say? The next town down the road?"

27

"No," Lazar said impatiently, "Lubnica is not the next town. Next is Boljevac, then Planinica. And then," he said triumphantly, raising his eyes to meet the German's, "only then, comes Lubnica."

The corners of the soldier's mouth twitched upward slightly at Lazar's evident feeling of major victory over the minor issue. He pointed at the rucksack.

"What do you have in there?"

Lazar opened the cloth bag and pulled out a lump of goat's milk cheese wrapped in paper and a hard end of blackish bread.

"Unwrap it."

He held out the gray chunk of cheese. "You are welcome to it, sir."

The German recoiled. "Ach, you imbecile! Break it."

Lazar grinned at him crookedly. He broke the cheese open and held up the pieces. "You see? Cheese inside, too."

The soldier tapped Lazar's papers impatiently against his thigh as Lazar fumbled with the rewrapping of his lunch. Then he slapped the documents into Lazar's hands. "All right. Be sure you do not slow your trip past the airfield."

"Thank you," Lazar said. *"Dobar dan.* Good day."

The soldier strode back to the motorcycle, his jackboots crunching the gravel road, and swung into the saddle.

As Lazar pedaled past, his eyes focused straight ahead, he heard the young soldier say to his partner, "Just another goat-cheese eater."

The other laughed darkly. "What did you think he had in the cheese? A camera?"

As the drumming of the motorcycle faded behind him, Lazar permitted himself a brief smile. He had a camera, all right. It was in his head.

The towns of Boljevac, Planinica, and Lubnica were little more than collections of stucco buildings sprinkled along the road, each with its church and town hall; each with its few badly-dressed, stone-faced old men and young boys and an occasional woman in traditional white. All of them stared somberly at the street as Lazar passed by. Staying free of trouble in these confused times depended mainly upon strictly minding one's business. A stranger of fighting age could very well be a Titoist, one of the Ustasha, or even Gestapo. Lazar passed through the three settlements without incident and stopped on a promontory overlooking a deep valley to eat his bread and cheese. Three kilometers eastward lay the outskirts of Zajecar.

As he pedaled down the last slope toward Zajecar, Lazar's alert eyes swept a scene of destruction below. To the west of town, he saw that the American bombers had turned the railroad terminal into a twisted ruin. Rails had been uprooted and blasted into a mass of warped and angular junk which was scattered about the bomb craters like clumsy jackstraws. An ill-assorted group of men were dismantling the charred wreckage of a dozen freight cars and feeding it to a growing bonfire near the battered stucco railroad station.

The directors of the repair operation wore the field gray of the Wehrmacht. That was interesting. He had expected the olive-brown uniforms of the Bulgarian troops who usually occupied this area. Following the plan he had worked out during the long miles since dawn, Lazar pushed on. He bounced through the sparsely-peopled streets on the west side of Zajecar, passed across the worn cobbles of the town square, and neared the railroad station. Minutes later, he could see the battered terminal beyond the shops that lined either side of the main street. Three blocks to go.

A helmeted German sergeant stepped from the shadow of

a tobacconist's shop and blocked Lazar's path with wide-set booted legs and a Schmeisser machine gun at the ready.

Lazar wobbled to a stop.

The German motioned with the muzzle of his gun. "Get off that thing," he barked. "You will come with me."

FOUR

Alone in his hospital room near Berlin, his head and face swathed in gauze, Erwin Buckler was trying to collect his thoughts. The earth had trembled last night. Through the bandages over his ears, Buckler had heard the thundering twenty kilometers distant. The R.A.F.'s Lancasters had been busy, and still more of Berlin had turned to flame. From the darkened hospital windows, the nurses had watched the glow fan along the south horizon. One of them had looked in briefly on Buckler, at what he estimated was about 3:00 A.M. Otherwise, he had been left alone. Who wanted to spend time with a man who was unable to see or even speak?

But the bandages didn't keep him from thinking. When he had first been transferred here from the poorly-equipped hospital in Belgrade, he was still gripped by a confusion of pain, hopelessness, hate—a dozen fears and angers.

The plastic surgeon the Luftwaffe had ordered here from Berlin had set to work grimly. Buckler remembered his little blond moustache and rimless pince-nez glasses, seen through a haze of pain, awhirl in a sea of anesthetic. Then the bandages had shut out the fearful distortions, and he slept.

The bitter alcohol on a cold thermometer placed between his numb lips awoke him at last.

"*Guten Morgen,* major." The nurse's voice was soft and reassuring. He tried to answer.

"*Nein, nein,*" she said quickly. "No motion of the facial muscles. It will not be too long, major. The doctor is to return Wednesday."

So he could only lie motionless on his back, staring into his eyelids while silence and pain and boredom rolled a kaleidoscope across his mind.

Number 401. That was the number he must never forget. No matter what else the war held for him, he would learn the identity of that cowardly pilot, and blast him forever from the air. And what else did he expect from the war? There was no denying that it had turned sour, though the Fuehrer did not seem to believe so. The rumors of Allied landings in France had reached even to the foot of Rtanj Mountain. But the rumors had proved false, of course. *Festung Europa,* the Fuehrer termed the Third Reich: Fortress Europe. The Americans and English were able to drop bombs on it, but that was not the same as breaching the wall.

And there were the victory weapons: the secret work at Peenemünde in the Baltic, and the feverish preparations near Zajecar which he, himself, had been assigned to safeguard.

32

Yet, when the floor of the hospital had shaken beneath his bed last night, Buckler had wondered how long victory would have to wait. How many bombs would fall before the mighty victory weapons could be put into action? In what he judged to be a predawn hour—the lowest ebb of a man's resistance—Erwin Buckler found a new thought woven through the jumble that kept him awake. Was it monstrously possible that all was already lost? That the V weapons were empty propaganda? That he was guarding part of an intricate hoax to keep hope alive when actually there was no hope?

That thought was too horrible. He rejected it and concentrated once again on the number that he would never forget. Number 401. He would contact Luftwaffe Intelligence the very hour he was released from this place of antiseptics and the endless sound of feet and wheels on corridor floors.

At nine-thirty that morning, the bandages were unwound. "Only a routine examination," the doctor's precise voice cautioned. "I am simply observing progress, major. It will be more days before you are released."

The gauze and cotton pulled free with little stabbing tugs. His face was stiff and raw.

"Are you able to open your eyes?"

The light was like sharp points driving into his head. He saw them as though through milky water.

"*Gut, gut.* Try not to move the face at all, major."

Buckler heard the nurse catch her breath sharply, and he squinted to bring her into focus.

"*Das ist alles,*" the doctor said quickly. "You may replace the bandages."

When he was wrapped in darkness once more, his hearing

seemed to be acute. He could hear the rustle of the nurse's uniform; every sharp click of the instruments as she cleared the tray.

And when they finally left him alone and closed the door to his room, he heard the doctor say quietly in the corridor, "You had best remove the mirror from his room, Fraulein."

Six hundred and fifty miles to the southwest, Lazar needed no mirror to tell him that he had become as grubby and charcoal-stained as the gang of peasants with whom he was now working to clear debris in the Zajecar railroad yard. His plan thus far had gone well. The only cost had been his bicycle and his forged identity papers. By now, the bike was no doubt the property of some German noncom, and the papers were being held with those of every other able-bodied man whom the Germans had been able to find in the area. Only when these drafted and unsmiling laborers had finished the clean-up job would they get their papers back. Here in occupied territory that was enough to hold them. A man without papers was a man in deep trouble.

Lazar, though, was not much concerned about the loss of his papers—or about his bicycle, either, for that matter. Its loss meant only that he would have to make his way back to Chetnik headquarters on foot, a matter of a couple of nights' hard walking and a day or two of hiding in the shelter of the scattered woods.

The Zajecar sentry had turned him over to the soldiers directing the work in the railroad yard. Lazar had worked into the night, joined the others around the soup kettle, and slept a few hours on the hard floor of a boxcar. Before dawn, he and the two dozen others in the group were prodded back to work.

Daylight brought more thin soup and the chance to stand

34

shivering around the smoky fire, toasting one side while the other took on the damp chill of the dawn air. During this break, he began to work on a brawny peasant from Lubnica, who was named Milan.

"Postaje hladno. It's getting cold, no?"

"Cold enough," muttered Milan.

Lazar kicked a stone disgustedly. "A man slaves to ready his field, then comes this."

Milan looked at him, then glanced around quickly before replying. "They took me right out of my field, too. Two days ago."

"Wheat?" Lazar asked.

"No, barley. How long do you think this will last?"

"Until the yard is clear enough for repairs to begin. A trainload of new ties and rails is already on the siding over there."

A German corporal walked past, his shoulders hunched against the chill and his eyes downcast. Milan waited until he was out of hearing. "Maybe it will not be many more hours. You can see they are not clearing the main track east. Just the spur track north into the mountains."

Lazar had noted this interesting fact ten minutes after he arrived. *"Zasto?* Why is that?" he said dully. "Don't supplies have to get through Rumania to the Russian Front?"

Milan studied Lazar, and Lazar stared into the fire, showing unconcern.

"You are not from here?" said Milan.

"No. Paracin."

"Then you have not heard the thunder in the mountains?" Milan's voice was low. "Thunder on a clear day, my friend. And I hear it all the way to Lubnica."

"Thunder on a clear day?" Lazar kept his voice flat. "Has no one seen what causes it?"

"You are a stranger, all right. It is as if the whole German Army was in the mountains up there. But there is only the railroad track and the road beside it. No other roads. On the mountains are few trees and they have strung mines that give warnings."

A whistle shrilled nearby. "Back to work!" a soldier shouted. "Rest is over! Back to work!"

The group around the fire groaned and muttered.

"Work with me," Lazar said to Milan. "Perhaps two barley farmers will work well together."

The big peasant grinned and willingly followed Lazar back to the tangled jumble of railroad ties he had been salvaging before the breakfast soup break.

"Do you hear the thunder in the hills often?" Lazar asked, after making certain no guard stood nearby.

"In the past days, yes."

"Are they dynamiting, do you think? Perhaps building something back in the hills?"

Milan shook his head. "Not explosions. A long rumble like—like the earth has begun to split in half."

"You two there!" a German guard shouted, unslinging his rifle menacingly. "Silence! Work!"

"Prisoners," Milan whispered. "Prisoners in our own country."

An hour after night had shut out the sight of the mountains, and cooking fires were glowing in the murky freight yard, Lazar slipped into the darkness and traded his short career as a railroad worker for that of a fugitive. He doubted that he would be missed for hours, if at all. There hadn't been one roll call during the time he had labored in Zajecar. Apparently the Germans felt that the impounded identity papers were security enough.

36

That didn't worry Lazar. During the long trek back to Chetnik headquarters, he would move through the open country by night and sleep under rocky overhangs and in the woods by day. But before striking off cross-country, he was determined to get as close as he possibly could manage to whatever it was that nested in the mountains. The burly peasant's information had been limited but significant. Lazar had toyed with the idea of staying in or near the Zajecar yards until the first train rolled up the repaired spur line. Perhaps he could have swung aboard unobserved. But he had discarded the idea when a transient detachment of black-uniformed SS troops had driven through the rail yard and set up a bivouac a half kilometer up the spur. There was no bluffing the SS. If you were caught, you were dead. Lazar's meager information was already too valuable, he decided, to risk capture. And coming across the mountains on foot, a man alone might have a better chance to see something worthwhile.

By midnight Lazar was nearing a location he felt could be the source of Milan's "thunder." He had been guided by native instinct, by a dramatic fold in the mountains that had suddenly produced a beautifully protected canyon, and by the fact that he had several times glimpsed the spur line and its paralleling road far below him through rifts in the rocky ridge along which he walked. The half-moon had risen. It gave enough light to silhouette the purple mountains against the lighter purple sky. Its cold glow had reflected from the distant rails twenty minutes ago. Though the spur line had since disappeared beyond the rolling ridge, Lazar knew the line had to follow the valley to his right.

Ahead, a few towering fir trees broke the monotony of the barren terrain. Here, Lazar decided, he would rest a moment. A man gets old, he thought, even though he won't admit it. He would stop a moment. Then he would cut directly east and take a good look into the canyon.

It was a matter of a half kilometer, he estimated. If he saw nothing, Milan was then at best an overly imaginative farmer; at worst, an impish liar who was now laughing at Lazar's disappearance. If he saw nothing, then OSS was as bad as Milan, with their conjuring of big projects out of little suspicions.

What did he himself expect? He honestly didn't know. There was only one way to find out. He left the shadow of the big pine, took five silent steps—and froze.

To his left—about ten meters, he judged—there was the noise of a hard object scraping on stone. Then, beneath an isolated group of small trees, a clattering in the blackness.

He held his breath, cursing his stupidity. The trees were a perfect cover for a fixed sentry post!

Then he let out his breath in a wheezy gust. The dim form of a deer moved into the moonlight, sniffed the air, and slowly turned its head toward him.

The deer stiffened. Lazar could feel its fear and well understand it. The muscles tensed, and the animal leaped gracefully forward, loping down the same shallow saddle Lazar intended to use as an approach to the deep valley just beyond. Its hoof beats faded, and Lazar moved out once again.

He could just make out a final insolent flick of the deer's white tail flag. Then, to his amazement, the distant fleeing animal disappeared in a shattering blast.

Lazar hit the ground hard. A concussion wave rammed his chest as he dropped, and rock fragments clinked across the open ground and tumbled through the pine branches behind him.

38

A mine!

Like gleaming silver fingers, two searchlight beams slashed wildly across the night from both sides of the saddle not five hundred meters ahead. Sharp commands in German rose over the fading echoes of the explosion.

Lazar was convinced. He scrambled back into the protecting darkness, gulped cold night air through a bone-dry mouth, and ran.

FIVE

Captain Edgar Tanner had been summoned to Wing Headquarters by scrambler phone. "Your tip on Zajecar panned
out," Major Fred Kelleher had told him crisply over the
wire. "We've planned a fairly high-level briefing at nineteen
hundred hours. Be here, will you?"

Kelleher's request was really an order, but Tanner
wouldn't have been kept away by weather far worse than
the spring rain now streaking the blacked-out windows of
the old villa that served as Wing HQ.

"Fairly high-level briefing" was an understatement. As
Tanner polished his steel-rimmed glasses with the tip of his
khaki tie, he squinted from his rear row seat around the
high-ceilinged library of the old villa. The gathering of
some twenty Wing and Air Division officers ran heavily to
majors and colonels, but in the front row gleamed the bald
head of Major General Carter Thiebold, flanked by the pre-

cisely barbered heads of his aides. Some contrast to the more informal officers back at Group, Tanner reflected.

Exactly at nineteen hundred, whip-thin and darkly scowling, Major Kelleher strode to the front of the room and faced the group, producing an instant silence.

"General Thiebold has asked me to thank all of you for your promptness, gentlemen." Kelleher's voice was sharp and precise. "We all have work that's got to be done, so I'll be brief and to the point." He nodded to the lowest-ranking man in the room.

"All right, lieutenant, lights please, and we'll have the first slide."

A click plunged the library into darkness, and Major Kelleher stepped aside as a map of Yugoslavia appeared on the brilliant silver square of the screen behind him.

"In southeastern Yugoslavia, there is a railhead named Zajecar. Right here, gentlemen." He tapped the screen with a pointer.

"Two weeks ago, a squadron of the 456th was sent on a strike against the Zajecar rail yard. A routine mission against increased rail traffic we thought was supplying the German eastern front. Twelve Liberators went in and only five came out. They ran into what we have since learned is probably the best Luftwaffe fighter squadron outside of Germany."

There was a stir of interest in the room. In the glow of the projector, Tanner could see that General Thiebold was no longer relaxed in his chair but now sat stiffly forward.

"We have identified this fighter unit as Kommando Boelcke. It's commanded by Erwin Buckler, a major with somewhere around fifty claimed victories. They're equipped with FW 190D's. Now why, gentlemen, would the Luftwaffe equip a crack fighter unit with the latest planes and station it in this remote corner of the world when Goering needs every fighter he can get his hands on to send against the Allies over Germany and Austria?"

He nodded toward the lieutenant. "Next slide, please." The screen was now filled with a high-altitude straight-down photograph of mountainous country surrounding the white buildings of a fair-sized town.

"This aerial photo was taken yesterday morning by P-38 photorecon at twenty thousand feet. The town is Zajecar. This—" he stretched the pointer across the screen— "confluence of waterways is the point in Zajecar where the Crna River coming in from the west joins the Timok River, which then flows northeastward into the Danube at the intersection of the Yugoslavian, Bulgarian, and Hungarian borders twenty-five miles northeast. Up here—to the northwest—is an area of deep folds and crevasses. This whitish streak is a rail spur and a parallel truck road winding into those mountains and then suddenly disappearing."

General Thiebold cleared his throat and rasped, "Kelleher."

"General?"

"What do you mean, disappearing? It simply ends in that canyon."

"Next slide, please," Kelleher said, by way of an answer. A view from a much lower altitude appeared, showing only the deep twisting valley in which the spur line terminated. "This is the canyon to which the general refers." The rubber tip of the pointer tapped the middle of the screen.

"Now look closely, gentlemen," Kelleher said. "The track *appears* to terminate in the canyon. But actually it continues straight into the hillside. This foliage at the 'end' of the track is artificial—and a good job, too. We sent in a second P-38 this morning with infrared film to confirm that.

42

No question about it—that spur line and the road beside it pass right into the mountain."

Murmurs swept the room. Tanner found that his fingers were tightly gripping the arms of his chair. Like everyone else, he silently cursed Kelleher for his obvious relish in this dramatic presentation. Get on with it, man!

Kelleher's voice spoke once again out of the darkness. "Ten days ago, OSS requested a ground reconnaissance of the Zajecar area. An agent was sent in by the Chetniks—"

"Chetniks?" someone interrupted. "I thought we were supporting Tito now. Policy changed a couple of months back."

"Except in eastern Serbia," said Kelleher, unruffled. "That's a holdout area for Mihailovic, the only territory where he has any influence now. Elsewhere we've had to shift support to Tito—he's much better organized and more effective. Except in the vicinity of Zajecar. There Mihailovic's man reported high-priority repairs on the spur line. Forced civilian labor, in fact, along with the Wehrmacht troops. He worked in the railyard himself for a day or two. Then he moved into the mountains where he'd heard a report of prolonged rumbling sounds. He penetrated to about here" —tap-tap of the pointer on the screen— "a mile or so from the end of the rail line."

Kelleher replaced the pointer on a pair of hooks on the wall. "All right, lieutenant, we'll have the lights again."

The sudden brilliance made Tanner blink rapidly until his eyes readjusted. A colonel with a face like a thoughtful eagle fixed Kelleher with a beady stare. "And just what did Mihailovic's man learn about your disappearing railroad, major?"

Kelleher locked his thumbs behind his back and paced across the front of the room. "He discovered that the area is protected by mines, warning devices, searchlights, and a very well dug-in unit of German troops."

"But the spur line," the colonel persisted. "What did he learn about that?"

"Nothing," Kelleher admitted. "He very nearly got himself killed by a mine, and he pulled out before he was caught. The spur line, we have decided, supplies some sort of research or manufacturing unit built under the east edge of the mountain."

" 'We?' Who's 'we'?" the colonel barked.

"Intelligence Section, Wing, working with Target Selection, Air Division," Kelleher said smoothly, and Tanner held back a grin. The colonel nodded and kept quiet.

"Apparently the Germans have managed to convert a large natural cavern and fit it with heavy concrete buttressed doors. I would imagine the place is at least as solid as the submarine pens at Saint Nazaire. And we haven't been able to touch them from the air."

"Nonsense!"

The challenge hung in the haze of blue cigar smoke that had filled the room. Heads turned and found the squat bulldog of a brigadier general who had contradicted Major Kelleher. Tanner recognized him immediately: General Harlan McClave, a former artilleryman who believed in the "creeping barrage" or "box barrage"—terms that meant total use of heavy explosives.

"Saturation bombing, gentlemen." McClave's face was as red as molded beef. "Hit 'em heavy and hit 'em much. No Mickey Mouse mountain cave is going to stand up under our two-thousand-pounders."

"Sounds sensible," General Thiebold put in. "That's not a reinforced sub pen we're talking about. That's a rock and dirt mountain."

"But mostly rock, general," Kelleher managed to get in, and Tanner could see that Kelleher didn't like the way the discussion was going.

"Send enough B-24's against that mountain," growled General McClave, "and there'll be nothing left but rubble. Won't matter what they're up to in there. It'll be junk when we're finished."

From the jumble of voices came the brass-hard words of General Carter Thiebold. "Gentlemen! Gentlemen. We appreciate your thoughts on this. And Major Kelleher, we thank you for your excellent briefing. You may return to your various headquarters, gentlemen. I thank you for your time, and you will get the final decision from Air Division just as rapidly as we can determine the best action to follow. Good night, Harlan," he said to General McClave in a lower voice. "Thanks for coming. I'll be in touch." An aide helped him into his heavy overcoat with its glittering double stars. The room began to clear.

Tanner worked his way to Kelleher's side. "What's your best guess on what they're up to in that mountain, Fred?"

Kelleher's thin mouth twisted in a grimace. "If you're asking me to guess, O.K., I will. Couldn't do it up there." He gestured toward the front of the room. "My feeling is that Hitler's got one more ace up his sleeve, Edgar. Something with a special engine—that's what's making those rumblings up there in the mountains. But this is all off the record. I'm only supposed to report facts—not guesses. I can't give opinions at these briefings unless someone asks for them."

"And tonight nobody did."

"General McClave had the opinions," Kelleher said tightly. "Maybe he's right. Let's hope so. Thiebold listens to him."

"Well, make sure McClave gets a complete set of recon photos," Tanner urged.

Kelleher looked at him curiously. "That's over four dozen photos."

"I know it is. I hope somewhere in the middle of them he'll realize how tight the bend is in the valley. Bombs don't drop straight down, Fred. And they don't go around corners, either."

SIX

The transport plane circled the fighter base at the foot of Rtanj Mountain, lost altitude, landed, and taxied to the flight line. The hot engines clanked to silence. The passenger door opened, and a Luftwaffe noncom laid it back against the fuselage.

A reception committee of half a dozen officers waited in a little semicircle outside the plane's exit. The noncom drew back into the fuselage, moving aside smartly for an officer who stepped blinking into the somber Yugoslavian spring drizzle. He stood framed in the doorway like an unbelievable surrealistic painting.

"Himmel!" one of the waiting officers muttered before he could control his words.

The tall officer in the doorway wore a mask of too-perfect skin stretched tightly over the frame of the facial bones. Near each ear, the grayish color faded to flat white blotches, which showed, on close examination, tiny stitch marks. The nose was perfectly molded, but the nostrils were neat round holes as if they had been precisely placed with a drill. The lips were well formed, but colorless. There were no eyebrows on the china-like mask, and no beard would ever grow again on the polished cheeks and ivory chin.

The best doctors in Berlin had done their work well, but they could not match nature. With his face carefully rebuilt into an expressionless model that represented the best of the plastic surgeon's ability, Major Erwin Buckler had returned to duty.

Within an hour, the great hall of the old monastery that served as headquarters was crowded with the officers of Kommando Boelcke, each trying to welcome their commander without showing obvious shock at his appearance. But Erwin Buckler was not fooled. He knew exactly what they felt. He had lived the horror himself when the nurse had finally given in to his shouted demands for a mirror.

They had made a monster of him.

"But Herr Major," the bull-like doctor with the gentle hands had protested, "if you could have seen what we had to work with. Wait, wait, I will get you the photographs."

"The devil with the photographs!" Buckler had shouted hysterically. "They can't bring back my face."

They had left him alone then. And in the stillness of the hospital room, he had slowly mastered his despair, put it down with a promise more bitter than his pledge to the Luftwaffe. He would be paid for this—paid with the explosions of B-24's in the icy winds of high altitude; paid with their twisted wreckage across the cruel mountains. He would get that bomber marked 401. He would seek it out and chop it into scrap with his pounding cannon. That would be his payment. And he hoped the war would be long

48

and that many American bombers would come. Because he wanted them to come to Zajecar to fall under his guns, and he knew that among them would be the B-24 with the crimson lightning-streaked tail marked 401.

"Stoltzman." He caught the eye of his personal aide, a lieutenant who reminded him of a trim Doberman Pinscher, alert, touchy, ready to bite.

"Sir?"

"I want Hauptmann Krafft here by mid-afternoon. It is a matter of urgency, and I will appreciate no excuses whatever."

Stoltzman disappeared immediately. Buckler forced himself through an uneasy lunch in the officers' dining hall. All eyes, he knew, were upon him, although quickly averted to avoid his gaze when he caught himself glancing about the huge, austere dining room with its murky vaulted ceiling. His eyes were cold blue chips, darting grimly in his frozen face. He ate mechanically, tasting nothing, forcing himself to swallow the sawdust sausage and stringy cabbage.

Shortly before fifteen hundred hours, Hauptmann Ludwig Krafft, his trench coat slick with rain, strode into the room that served as Buckler's office off the great dining hall. He must have been briefed by Stoltzman on Buckler's appearance, Buckler noted, because he showed no reaction at all as he saluted.

"Herr Major. I am glad you are able to return to duty."

"*Ja,*" Buckler replied tightly. "That I am able to do. To fly. To fight. That is almost enough. Tell me, have you managed to improve the anti-aircraft defenses since I have been away?"

As Buckler had expected, Krafft bristled. As a Wehrmacht officer he resented being outranked by a Luftwaffe man, and therefore being answerable to him. And Krafft was touchy about his assignment. He had been given good guns—new 88's—but he had been assigned no experienced gunners. "You must understand that defense of the homeland has first priority," had been the reply to his protest. "It is a miracle that we can supply the guns. The gunners you must train yourself."

The Zajecar home guard was pitiful. The excellent radar gun sights remained a complete mystery to them in spite of endless training hours by his own best non-commissioned officers.

But Krafft knew that Major Buckler, the hideous plaster mask that Major Buckler was now, was in no mood to hear about the problems of anti-aircraft defense.

Buckler's question still hung in the chilly, cell-like office with its desk and three chairs, stone floor, and chart-filled plaster walls.

"I am replacing the worst home guard gun crews with new crews of my own unit," Krafft said. "This procedure will thin out the defense perimeter around the installation, but I am certain our major danger is from the air. The only attempted penetration of the perimeter was by a deer some weeks ago."

"And did the deer get through?" Buckler asked sarcastically.

"It was blown up by a mine." Buckler's lips drew back in a humorless smile as Krafft obviously changed the subject. "You were informed of the American reconnaissance flights? Very high, except one pass, and very fast. They use a fighter plane with two fuselages, a strange-looking plane."

"It was a P-38," Buckler said, "called Blitzen. Lightning. Obviously taking photographs. We can expect further attention from the Fifteenth Air Force, Herr Krafft." His eyes glittered. "Let them come. Kommando Boelcke is ready,

50

and I have arranged further entertainments for their fighter cover."

"Fighter cover?"

"Of course. You do not for a minute believe they will return without fighter escort after losing seven out of twelve planes. I have managed to have a group of Messerschmitt 109's transferred to Bileca on the Adriatic coast between us and the American bases at Foggia. They are green pilots, for the most part, but they have only one assignment."

"To eliminate the American fighter escort."

"*Nein*, simpler than that. They have only to make the Americans drop their auxiliary fuel tanks."

Buckler picked up a dispatch sheet from his desk and snapped it with his forefinger. "Has this news reached you yet? It is the schedule of the first test of the new weapon."

Krafft was obviously startled, and Buckler's blank face hid his own delight.

"A test? When?" the ground officer asked.

"On Monday at thirteen hundred hours. This warm front will clear and the weather will be excellent. A radio-controlled Fieseler Storch will be the target. You saw it as you drove past the flight line on your way here."

"I thought it was a liaison plane. There have been rumors that high-ranking officials would visit the project."

"There are always those rumors. No, Krafft, upon the fate of that target plane could depend the future of the Reich." He couldn't resist the dramatic phrase, but as he said it, he knew Krafft was more amused than inspired. Miserable mud slogger. Krafft was a career officer of the worst type: his loyalty lay with the army rather than with the Fuehrer. And he had no imagination at all.

Far westward in the mist and light rain of the same early

51

June warm front, there was no lack of imagination at 456th Group Headquarters.

"I can almost write the strike report now, Marv," Captain Tanner said morosely to First Lieutenant Marvin Pilster, his assistant chief of intelligence. " 'All bombs struck within a thousand yards of the target. No visible damage.' " General McClave certainly must have done some heavy talking at Air Division, but I still think a standard attack will be a fiasco."

"And the losses," Pilster said. "What does your crystal ball tell you about that?"

"Well, not so bad this time. We'll have fighter escort."

"When's this big event to take place?"

"Air Division says go when the weather clears. According to Meteorology, that'll be Monday the fifth. The whole group, with two squadrons of P-51's as fighter escort. Flak shouldn't be bad, but those FW's. . . ."

Meteorology Section was accurate, and in the damp hour before Monday's dawn, Tanner found himself saying almost the identical words to the air crews assembled in the headquarters briefing room.

". . . flak over the target shouldn't be any worse than before, but those FW's are still loaded for bear. Four cannon and two machine guns each. You've already been told about your fighter escort. We've routed you around the flak areas to and from the target. According to current information, there are no other fighter bases in range of your route. So you'll have a clean trip in and out. The only fly in the ice cream is right at the target area—that fighter group at Rtanj Mountain."

Tanner's eyes swept over the group of flyers jammed on the narrow benches in the stuffy room. They were an independent bunch, these combat flyers. In the air, they looked pretty much the same, huddled in their brown sheepskin flying suits, but at briefings it was another story. Directly in front of Tanner sat a crew wearing flaming red scarves. Behind them, a moustached pilot hunkered on his bench in a Dartmouth football sweater. Marty Fields. Across the aisle the enlisted men of Stafford's crew had each gotten hold of a pair of R.A.F. flying gauntlets which they were now wearing, the flaring cuffs reaching to their elbows. They listened solemnly to the briefing.

Stafford's crew. With the possible exception of the replacement nose gunner who had arrived a few days before, they still had that disturbing air about them.

It was for the new gunner and the other replacements that Tanner said, "If any of you new men aren't sure of escape procedures, be sure to see me immediately after the briefing." He checked his notes one more time. "Questions, anyone? All right, then. Good luck, and here's Colonel Sarmondyke."

The Commander of the 456th Bomb Group climbed up on the platform as Tanner stepped down. He was a six-foot-two ex-lacross star from the Johns Hopkins University. Four years in the Air Force, first as an aviation cadet in the thirties, then quickly up the ladder to the command of a heavy bomber group, had touched his temples with premature gray. His hard hazel eyes seemed to find everyone in the room at once and to give each man a sudden jolt of determination.

Stafford felt it, too, and shifted his bulk on the bench. With this man leading us, he found himself thinking, I might make it through this day after all.

"You've heard the scoop on rendezvous, initial point, bomb run and all the rest. I know that you'll do the customary fine piece of work you're beginning to get famous for."

Colonel Sarmondyke paused, paced slowly across the platform, turned, and again faced his men.

"Now I'll tell you why we're taking the entire group, fifty-two heavy bombers, into Yugoslavia today. In that valley near Zajecar"—he pointed a thick forefinger at the map on the wall behind him—"right here, as Captain Tanner told you, is what we suspect is an underground factory. According to our best intelligence, the Germans are probably working on some sort of new propulsion system. For what, we frankly don't know. But it could be any of a number of things: a new fighter plane engine; some new sort of tank, perhaps. Whatever it is, our job is to plaster that valley. I want you bombardiers to hit your pinpoint, and you bombagators look sharp, now. Drop your bombs the exact instant you see the lead ship in your element drop his. A delay of even a second can make your whole bomb load ineffective. This is a very narrow target area."

And that, Stafford thought, is just why this mission could be a bust. Their attack technique was designed for mass bombing of large target areas. Sure, it was called "pinpoint" bombing, but the newspapers and magazines back home had a rather glorified view of just what that meant.

"With the Norden bombsight, you can drop a bomb in a pickle barrel from twenty thousand feet," a bombardier was supposed to have said. And Stafford guessed you could. But every plane in the 15th Air Force didn't carry one of these bombsights; in fact, only the lead and deputy lead bombers in each element carried even a bombardier. In the rest of the planes, the navigator doubled as bombardier, and his job over the target was to toggle all the bombs in salvo the instant the lead bombardier dropped his. In theory, the lead plane and its bombsight smacked the "pinpoint," which often was a tiny shed or a switch house in the middle of a vast railroad yard, and the drop pattern of the other bombers flattened the entire target.

At Zajecar, Stafford suspected, this technique might not be worth a hoot.

"So hold your formations tight, gentlemen," Colonel Sarmondyke finished. "And you gunners, make your bursts count. This could be a rough one. Good luck, and good bombing."

"What I don't like about flying," said Terrible Cochran fifteen minutes later, as Stafford's crew checked out their flying gear, "is all this infernal dressing. First the underwear, then the electric bunny suit, then the winter O.D.'s. Then the sheepskin pants, then the flying boots, then the sheepskin jacket—"

"And the Mae West," Si-Si Charles chimed in, "and the parachute harness, the helmet, the anti-flash goggles, the electric gloves, the leather gloves, the oxygen mask, the flak helmet, and the flak vest."

"You forgot the GI shoes you gotta carry in case you bail out," added Nick Pastore, "and the parachute pack you drag everywhere in the plane."

"A walking Army-Navy Store," Morry Flax put in glumly. "So let's walk."

Si-Si, Terrible, Hunky, Nick, and Morry headed for the door of the parachute supply building. Morry looked back.

"You O.K., Eddie?"

Corporal Edward L. Jarman, the new nose gunner, wasn't sure he wanted to be called "Eddie." In prep school, and before, it had been "Ted." But maybe "Eddie" would be better, at that. It sounded a little tougher, and he could use all the toughness the other crew members would credit him with. They had flown twenty-eight missions together, but he was as green as a spring apple. The others didn't seem to resent it. They had simply acknowledged his presence when he had come in by truck three days ago, and then they had gone on about their endless business of improving the tent that was home, and playing an interminable game of gin rummy. If Pastore ever collected the paper winnings they recorded in a tattered notebook, he'd be able to buy his own airplane.

Before Eddie Jarman had come in from the replacement pool, Stafford's crew had flown four missions with various nose gunners from other crews who had volunteered to fill in for the wounded and hospitalized Sandy Sanderson. Easy missions, Morry Flax had told Eddie. Northern Italy: a rail yard, two bridges, and a German motor pool.

Zajecar promised to be something else, and Eddie was scared. His legs were weak, and he stumbled as he went through the doorway into the soggy dawn, the mud sucking at his clumsy flying boots. The sky hung heavy and gray as bread pudding, but a golden line along the eastern horizon forecast clear air over the Adriatic. Eddie shuddered. They would go. His prayers for bad weather had gone unanswered.

A chunky hand grabbed his shoulder, and he turned into Stafford's broad stony face.

"Some trip for your first one. Just show us what you can do. That's all it takes."

The big pilot moved on, frozen-faced, leaving Eddie with a new thought. The other crew members were right. Jesse Stafford did seem like a man with more than one problem at a time.

Eddie ducked aboard through the bomb bay, the cold metal familiar under his gloved fingers, and climbed to the flight deck.

"Nobody in the nose on take-off," Stafford had told him

during their one brief talk. "That's one of my standard rules. Another is that if I ever give the signal to bail out, you go. No heroics, no riding her down with somebody who can't jump. And use those guns, but no long bursts. We don't carry replacement barrels."

The flight deck behind the pilot's compartment was crowded. Si-Si hunched on his little stool on the right side of the deck between his big liaison radio set and the stack of tuning units up the rear wall. On the bench along the left wall, Eddie slumped miserably beside Skinny Ennis. Hunky Molnar stood in the entrance hatchway beneath the upper turret that took up the space in the middle of the flight deck area.

The putt-putt muttered in its little niche below them, generating power for the lights and electric engine starters. The bomber was cold and smelled of gasoline, oil, and airplane. All Air Force airplanes smelled like this, Eddie thought. A strange nostril-grabbing savor that made you tense with excitement and a little numb, too. That was the fear part of it. It was always there, even on a training ride.

The grumblings of the newly started engines sent tremors through Eddie that were more than vibration. The rear hatch slammed hollowly. Morry Flax pushed through the narrow catwalk supports in the bomb bay and squeezed between Eddie and Skinny Ennis on the flight deck bench. Hunky Molnar hit a switch on the deck's aft bulkhead and the corrugated bomb bay doors rolled shut.

They taxied heavily along the field's paved perimeter. Eddie eyed the dark olive tiers of fat five-hundred pound bombs gleaming just behind the open flight deck entrance. That was the real thing back there—not little hundred-pound "blue-streak" practice bombs filled with sand and smoke markers. Not ten feet away, three tons of heavy demolition bombs packed with supercharged RDX waited to blast a hole in the Yugoslavian mountains.

The plane pitched sluggishly as Stafford hit the brakes. They crouched on the taxiway, third in a line of dozens of winged whales, their propellers silver discs in the weak dawn light; their muffled thunder rolling to the low hills on the distant fringes of the Foggian plain.

From the tower between the hangars, a flare streaked aloft, burst into a bright green ball, smoking on its drifting parachute.

"We go," said Ennis in Eddie's ear.

The lead B-24 turned onto the runway. Its propeller discs smoothed, and the engines howled above the grouped mutters of the bombers along the taxiway. The first B-24 rolled faster, grew smaller, finally lifted at the far end of the black runway and began a distant shallow turn.

The second bomber roared after the first, then Stafford let off his brakes with a lurch. 401 swung her teeth into the wind. Her engines deafened Eddie, and he felt the bomber lunge forward beneath him. It was illogical that such a ponderous conglomeration of men and metal could possibly gain the air.

The runway rushed past Si-Si's window. Tremors of accelerating power ran through the fuselage. Half-felt impacts told Eddie the Liberator was riding light now, her main gear pounding the shock stops.

Stafford eased the nose wheel off. The wings took hold, stiffened. The undulating bounces of the runway smoothed momentarily, then they skated across the washboard of the previous plane's turbulence that hung over the runway like invisible rapids.

And after long seconds, 401 found glassy air. She climbed eagerly into the rising sun, and Hunky Molnar's

58

voice shouted the raucous notes of some obscure Hungarian song he had picked up in the gritty canyons of Pittsburgh.

The group formed into a combat box over the western Adriatic, a tightly stepped formation that afforded maximum arcs of fire for the gunners.

Eddie had followed Skinny Ennis through the crawlway beneath the right side of the flight deck into the nose compartment. Eddie squeezed into his turret, flipped the power switch, and gripped the control yoke gingerly. Strange up here . . . He fought an urge to keep checking over his shoulder to make sure the rest of the plane was still following him.

He moved the two-handled control, and the turret inched to the left. Slanting the yoke back toward him brought the guns' twin black snouts up past eye-level, probing the air above him. Little wisps of vapor trailed across the clear blue up here, lots of them. Eddie plugged in his mike with rubber fingers. "Note to pilot. Something's up above us."

"What o'clock?" Stafford's hard voice rapped.

"One o'clock, high." The words sounded odd, although Eddie had said them often enough back at gunnery school.

"Stafford to crew. We've picked up our escort. Those are our P-51 Mustangs. I want all gunners in their turrets as of now. Check your guns, and look sharp. We'll hit the Yugoslav coast in fourteen minutes. I know there are no fighters between us and Serbia, but we'll play it safe."

Near Bileca, just twenty miles inland from Yugoslavia's Adriatic shore, a radar screen danced with a fascinating array of green-white blips, and the German sergeant took his eyes off of it long enough to smack a fat red button with his palm. In response, klaxon horns honked frantically.

The pilots of the new squadron had moved in four days

before, and more than a few of them had come straight from flight training deep in Germany. They made up in eagerness what they lacked in experience. Their 1150-horsepower Daimler-Benz engines barked, backfired blue smoke that was whisked away in prop blast, then moaned smoothly. Forty-three Messerschmitts screeched off the rough field, three at a time, blasted low across the clustered buildings of Bileca, then clawed for altitude and the blinding concealment of brilliant sun.

SEVEN

Jesse Stafford no longer knew how he would react to aerial combat. The four missions his group had flown since their close call at Zajecar had brought up inaccurate flak, but no fighters. He hadn't been put to the test, and that worried him.

And the rest of the crew worried him. He was sure they had quickly filled in the new guy—Eddie—on the trick Jesse had pulled to get them out of the bag on the Zajecar mission. But how did they really feel about it? A good officer wasn't supposed to care. "You're not in a popularity contest," they had drummed into his aviation cadet class. "A bomber pilot is a commander. Your plane comes first, then your crew. You come last."

The gunmetal-blue coast of Yugoslavia far below them drifted into view precisely on schedule, waves breaking whitely against its rocky shore.

Jesse flipped the selector switch and took a deep drag of pure oxygen. They had snapped on their clumsy masks a few minutes ago as they drummed past the ten-thousand-foot mark. The oxygen cleared his head and jacked him out of his depression.

He moved the oxygen selector back to auto and pressed the switch of his throat mike. "Check your guns."

Nick let go immediately with a burst that Jesse felt through the control column. Then the single waist guns cut loose, Hunky Molnar on one, and Si-Si, who had already moved back to his combat station, on the other. The tail guns sounded remotely, and were drowned by the crashing of the top turret .50's almost over Jesse's head.

"Pilot to nose. Check 'em, Jarman."

Eddie's voice was scratchy. "There's something else up there."

Stav jabbed Jesse's ribs and pointed to the command radio set. Jesse flipped his headset selector switch and picked up the tail-end of a P-51 transmission.

". . . in the sun. Two dozen ME's."

"Roger, Red Flag," another American fighter pilot's voice answered, then, "Flag leader to pennants. Get 'em!"

"Messerschmitts? Here?" said Stav.

Jesse thumbed his mike. "Pilot to crew. Stay off the intercom except to report attacks. We've got more than Mustangs out there." He hunched forward against his belt. His gloved left thumb blocked out the ball of the sun, and he found them: a distant line of hornets dropping out of the glare on the P-51 formation that was scattering five thousand feet above the lumbering B-24's. Jesse hit the mike again. "Get those flak vests and steel helmets on."

The bombers instinctively closed their formations, and the air got lumpier as the slipstreams of the leading B-24's merged into invisible rapids. Jesse stole an anxious look upwards, both hands fighting to keep the gyro compass centered and the bank indicator dead level. Little silver flashes dropped behind the Mustang escort. They had jettisoned their extra fuel tanks. That was bad, and cold perspiration broke out along Jesse's spine. How far could the P-51's shepherd them toward Zajecar now?

"Messerschmitt eleven o'clock high. . . ."

The voice belonged to Morry Flax. There it was, two thousand feet above them, diving steeply, showing only its head-on silhouette. It was an ME, all right. No mistaking those offset radiators under each wing.

The oncoming fighter began winking brightly, its outboard cannon and nose machine guns firing way out of range.

"Green and scared," said Morry dryly.

"Like me," Eddie's voice quavered, and nervous laughter rippled though the ship.

Morry's .50's cut loose, and Jesse jumped even though he'd been waiting for it.

"Come on, Eddie. Get in it!"

"I can't. He's too high for me."

Tracers from a dozen guns of the formation reached for the Messerschmitt. Too many tracers. He flipped over and half-rolled straight down in a long arc. Before he dropped out of sight below the nose, Jesse caught a glimpse of the markings on his plane. Mottled green on the upper surfaces; light blue underneath.

"Didn't I see red and yellow stripes around his fuselage aft of the cockpit?" he asked Stav. "That's a Reichsverteidigung I.D. band; home defense. They must have thrown this outfit down here in one heck of a hurry. We've got 'em worried."

63

"The feeling's mutual," said Stav.

A silver Mustang, its rudder checkerboarded yellow and black and its wings tipped with bright chrome yellow, dropped out of the battle overhead. The Mustang howled across the face of the thundering bomber boxes like a hungry hawk. Far below, the lone Messerschmitt zoomed back into sight. The Mustang swung across the bottom of its dive, the gleaming nose seeking its target. Thin white smoke streamers told Jesse the Mustang pilot had tripped his six machine guns.

He was good. The Messerschmitt staggered, skittered to the left, and plunged toward the Montenegran mountains. A spark under its cowling ballooned into a quick flare as the stricken fighter pulled its tail of oily smoke into a final flash in the woods far below.

The P-51 completed the zoom the Messerschmitt had begun and climbed back into the fighter battle that now ranged over a five-mile area above the bombers.

"Bijelo Polje dead ahead," Skinny Ennis reported. They were halfway to target.

An ME-109 exploded in front of the bombers, appearing from nowhere and rocking the lead bomber element with the shock wave of its sudden destruction. A shower of hot debris whistled among the Liberators. No one saw the pilot.

"Who got him?"

"Not us. I never saw the guy."

"Then start looking sharp!" Jesse snapped at the hesitant voice. Whose was it? Eddie frantically swiveling his Emerson turret under Jesse's nose? Terrible Cochran back in the lonely air rush beneath the big elevators?

"There goes a Mustang," Hunky said from his waist gun. "High at nine o'clock."

Through his side window, Jesse watched the Mustang

spiral tightly downward, out of control. *"Bail,"* he heard himself say to the unseen pilot, and he checked to be sure the mike button on the control yoke wasn't depressed. *"Come on, get out."* Now he thumbed the button. "Did he get out, Nick? I lost sight of him."

"No." Silence, then: "Wait, he's out. Chute opened just before she hit."

Suddenly the sky was clear of the bullet-nosed German fighters. The Mustangs reformed high above the bombers and resumed their zig-zag ranging across the big formation.

The fight had been brief. But Jesse knew the enemy hadn't been scared off; Luftwaffe fighter pilots pulled out only to refuel, or rearm, or because they were ordered off. The fight was too short to have exhausted their gasoline or ammo.

"What do you make of it?" asked Stav behind his green-tinted goggles.

"They did their job. You saw those wing tanks let go."

"How long can the Mustangs stay with us now?"

"With internal tanks only, they're good for something like nine hundred miles. That's about the distance to the target and back, but they used up a lot of juice on those Messerschmitts."

"Looks like a lonely trip to the mountains," said Skinny.

"Oh, there'll be someone to meet us," Si-Si put in brightly. And that shut them all up. The monotonous drone of the engines wrapped each man in his own thoughts.

The first lone Messerschmitt that had attacked the B-24's had done Jesse a major favor. The apprehension that had made today's take-off so difficult had left him. His hands were steady; his mind centered on the mission. He had passed a barrier, and he knew it. Now it didn't matter what the crew thought. They had a professional for a pilot.

He squinted at the climbing sun. It should be high enough for good strike photos when they reached the target.

The day had begun well before sun-up for Major Erwin Buckler. There was no stubble to shave, and he reached his office before any of his pilots appeared in the monastery's shadowed great hall. He forced down the hot, flat-tasting coffee Stoltzman brought him, then took particular delight in calling Ludwig Krafft's personal field phone number. He could picture Krafft bumbling about for the phone in the darkness of his Zajecar headquarters room.

"*Ja, Ja. Hier Hauptmann Krafft.*"

"*Hier Buckler.* The test is set for eleven this morning. There will be a group from Berlin arriving at nine-thirty."

"But we went over this yesterday, Herr Major."

"I told you I would give you confirmation. The dispatch reached me just a short time ago." It had reached him at midnight, but he had decided to begin the day by waking Krafft. "We will have the Storch airborne at ten minutes before eleven. Have your anti-aircraft units been notified?"

"Of course." Krafft's tone was snappish, then he caught himself and added, "But I will be sure to confirm it."

Buckler pulled back his mouth in a one-sided smile. One of his two pleasures in life was baiting Hauptmann Krafft. The other? Let the Americans come again. They would know the other.

The graceful four-engined Focke-Wulf Courier swept out of the northwest precisely at nine-twenty-eight, and it circled the fighter field, flashing against the hulk of Rtanj Mountain as the sun caught its slender wings. The sleek transport made its final turn smoothly and settled as lightly as a snowflake.

No ordinary pilot, that, Buckler observed. He nodded to

66

the five officers he had chosen to greet the visitors from Berlin, and they strode smartly across the new grass.

The first officer out of the Courier was a compact little oberst—a colonel—and it was he, himself, who had opened the door and secured it. That set off the instinctive signal in Buckler's head that this was no ordinary inspection team.

"Major Buckler? I am Oberst Vogel. This test is to be on schedule, I trust? We have only a limited time to spend here today."

"Of course, sir. May I present Hauptmann Webel, my chief of operations; Oberleutnants Schneider, Pichler, and Hollesch, my squadron commanders; and Leutnant Stoltzman, my aide."

He made the introductions by reflex, giving more attention to the scene unfolding behind Oberst Vogel. A frozen-faced Generalmajor was descending the steps from the plane now, his Luftwaffe uniform spotless and pressed to knife edges.

"Generalmajor Ebbing," Oberst Vogel announced. Buckler executed a tight military salute, his fingers extended at his cap visor.

The third officer to debark wore the Iron Cross with diamonds. He was older than Vogel or Ebbing, his eyes deepset in brown wrinkles.

"Generaloberst von Schalluck," Oberst Vogel said, a whip-crack in his voice. Buckler ramrodded his spine, rapped his heels together with a satisfying clack, and saluted again.

Surely this must be the entire delegation—a full general, a brigadier general, and a colonel. Still they waited.

Then Erwin Buckler got the shock of his life. Down the steps came an immensely fat officer, his high-peaked cap surmounting a face of jowls, a fleshy nose, a chubby jutting chin. His wide, thin-lipped mouth was pulled back grimly at the corners. The eyes were sunken black coals under heavy lids beneath a broad forehead with just the suggestion of eyebrows. It was a soft face with hard eyes.

The officer was broad but not particularly tall. His sparkling white dress uniform was beautifully fitted to his unmilitary figure, the shoulder boards gleaming, the flaring lapels faced with bright crimson silk.

Buckler's arm shot out stiffly in the Nazi salute. Reaching the bottom step and dropping half a meter to the grass with a muffled grunt was Reichsmarschall Hermann Goering, Commander-In-Chief of the Luftwaffe and second in political power only to Adolf Hitler himself.

Goering returned Buckler's salute without much formality, simply bending his arm upward from the waist, palm out. "Are we too late for a second breakfast, von Schalluck? The food on the plane was abominable."

Von Schalluck looked pained. *"Bitte . . ."*

Buckler nodded to Stoltzman, who trotted eagerly toward a telephone in the administration hut.

"We will go by automobile to our headquarters building, up there on the hillside." Buckler turned and pointed to the distant monastery, chalk-white against the higher hills beyond it. "After I have outlined the essentials of our part of the morning's activities, we will return here for the actual demonstration."

He was eager to see it himself. What he had learned about the project in the past few days was encouraging almost beyond belief.

"You have seen the weapon, major?" Goering asked Buckler as they neared his automobile, an open Mercedes touring car.

"Nein. Only the installation personnel themselves are

68

permitted. I am responsible for aerial defense only—and the target plane." He slipped an anxious glance down the flight line where a squad of mechanics readied the gawky high-winged monoplane that was to serve as the test target.

Buckler dismissed his staff commanders and climbed into the front seat of his open staff car with Oberst Vogel. Goering was already comfortably seated in the center of the wide back seat, flanked by Generalmajor Ebbing and Generaloberst von Schalluck. The engine purred, and the car pulled out of the operations area, leaving in its wake an unnoticed and winded communications noncom frantically waving a message form.

There next followed a series of delays that drove Buckler almost to the point of fist-pounding fury.

"Tell me, major," Goering rasped in his ear as they reached the narrow lane that linked the monastery with the Zajecar-Lubnica road, "are there any historic churches in the vicinity?"

"Churches?" Had he heard the Reichsmarschall clearly?

"Where one may find perhaps paintings, perhaps an interesting icon, you understand?"

Now Buckler did understand, indeed. Goering's private art collection was already second to none in the Reich.

"The test, Reichsmarschall—"

"The test, major, is not scheduled for another hour and fifteen minutes."

Buckler was certain he felt a subtle pressure from Oberst Vogel's elbow. Apparently the Reichsmarschall had made up his mind.

"There is an old church a few meters beyond Rtanj Mountain. . . ."

The murals were beautiful, still bright after a century of damp Balkan winters and mountain mists. But they had been painted on solid masonry. Goering kicked one of the old pews in frustration. "They have been permitted to carry away and hide everything of value. Our occupation troops were extremely careless here, von Schalluck."

Avoiding comment, the aging generaloberst flicked out his arm and studied his wrist watch. "It is ten-twenty, Herr Reichsmarschall."

On the return trip, Buckler's driver managed to lose another ten minutes by mistakenly taking the wrong fork and heading westward for more than three kilometers before Buckler angrily told him to turn around and concentrate on one of two things: the right road or a court-martial.

Then, with the airfield at last in view below them, Goering's pudgy fingers tapped Buckler's shoulder. "Halt the car. Halt the car here."

With Generalmajor Ebbing leading the way, the Reichsmarschall stepped ponderously off the running board and strode to the edge of the road. He stood facing the broad valley below them. "Beautiful," he murmured. "It must be caught on canvas. I will commission my personal artist to capture this exact view. Vogel, make a note of this location, will you?"

"*Ja,* Reichsmarschall. Of course." He scrabbled about in his blouse pockets.

Buckler stared at the tableau, sweat glistening on his forehead. Goering was simply unbelievable. His mind seemed to leap from one subject to the next; from his stomach to art treasures to the beauties of nature. And at a time like this.

Nervously, he checked his watch. Ten-forty. He looked up, inadvertently catching Vogel's eye. The nervous little oberst gave him a hint of a hopeless shrug.

Far down in the valley a little dragonfly trundled from

70

the long line of fighters. The target plane was being guided into take-off position. Buckler could hear its engine. . . .

No, the sound was coming from around the next bend. A motorcycle careened into sight, its rider hunched low. The cycle slewed to a stop in a rattling spray of gravel. The driver leaped free, letting his machine simply fall to the ground. He ran toward Buckler, saluting loosely as he came.

"Couldn't find you, major . . . just spotted you with binoculars from the field. . . ." The man gasped for breath. "Bombers. The Americans. They are on the way."

Buckler fought to keep his voice steady. "To arrive when? Didn't radar tell you when?"

The dispatch rider tugged at his tight jacket collar. "Within a half hour on their present course."

A nightmare.

"Do you have a radio on that thing?"

"*Nein,* major."

Of course not. No such luck on this morning of idiocy.

"You must get back to the field immediately. Stop the test."

The cyclist was staring past him to the valley floor. Buckler whirled. The Storch rose lightly from the fighter field, its little engine buzzing.

"Incredible imbeciles!"

A rising thunder of many engines drowned the lightplane's hum. The Focke-Wulfs parked in neat gray rows wore silver discs as the men of Kommando Boelcke scrambled under the orders of their individual squadron commanders.

"But not all of them are imbeciles," Buckler muttered with silent thanks to his three squadron leaders.

Vogel grabbed his arm. "We must take cover, major."

"Nonsense!" Goering's voice was firm; commanding. "The target is miles distant. Simply move the automobile under those trees. We will remain here."

For the first time, Goering sounded like an officer.

EIGHT

The Mustangs stuck it out to the frazzled limit of their range. Then Eddie Jarman watched them sink below him, a swiftly plunging swarm of silver darts. They wheeled around the far side of Rtanj Mountain, broke into the valley in three widely-spaced waves, and laced the fighter field with flaming puffs of dust and ricocheting tracers.

The low-level pass left an ammunition shed erupting brilliant flashes.

"Kiss the Mustangs goodbye," said Stav. "They're heading west."

Jesse nodded. "And they'll be going home on their gas fumes. O.K., now, everybody look sharp. I don't see many FW's down there. How about it, Nick?"

"Dozen, maybe. Probably down for repairs."

"Then the rest of them are somewhere up here."

73

"Hey, what's that!" Morry's voice was high with excitement.

"What o'clock?" Jesse demanded gruffly. "Call them for the rest of us, will you?"

"Two o'clock high. Some kind of a little airplane out there."

Stav pushed his face close to his side window. "Maybe Terrible could identify it. He's good at that."

Jesse pressed his mike button. "Terrible, duck out of that tail turret and take a look out of the right waist window."

For a minute or two, silence on the intercom. Then: "You won't believe it, but that's a Feiseler Storch. A German lightplane. Flopping all over the sky. The guy must be out of oxygen."

"*What* guy?" Morry said. "There's no pilot in that thing—"

"And it's coming straight at us!" Si-Si shouted.

The Storch staggered into the fringes of the big combat box, thus far unfired upon. But the idea that it was making some sort of attack suddenly occurred to a dozen gunners at once. The bright tracers reached out, and behind each tracer flew three armor-piercing incendiaries. The yawing Storch simply disintegrated, flying into bits and pieces. The engine and long-legged landing gear sailed down in a long tumbling curve. A wing flipped over and over until it disappeared below.

"You're right, Morry," Jesse said. "No pilot." That was something to think about.

But not for long.

"Bogies. Seven o'clock high." Terrible was back in his turret.

"How many?"

"At least fifty."

74

"Going to be rough."

"Off the air, Nick," Jesse growled. "I want a tight crew from here on in."

"Seven Focke-Wulfs coming straight and level from six o'clock," Terrible rapped. He slid his thumb off the mike button. That finished the words. Now it was life or death.

The fighters drilled into the rear of the bomber box, and every tail gunner in range, Terrible realized, felt they were after him personally. He nudged his control handle and inched the glowing ring of the gunsight toward the center fighter in the rapidly growing line.

Their wings began to wink, and Terrible triggered thunder back at them.

The tracers streaked out, danced around the onrushing fighters—his tracers, and the fire from ten more B-24's.

The Focke-Wulfs broke off in a zoom, and flame tipped the guns of upper turrets all through the formation.

No hits, no errors.

Twenty-eight wing cannon flashed like strings of firecrackers. Something thudded into the tail assembly. Terrible clamped his triggers. Short bursts . . . Hard to remember when you were about seven-eighths scared to death.

Five of the second fighter wave broke away upward, exposing their armored bellies to the top turrets. The other two decided to plunge downward in a pass at the bottom bomber element. Nick's guns hammered, and white-yellow flame flared at the muzzles of the ball turret guns on Jesse's side of the formation. The leading FW's cockpit canopy dissolved, and its left elevator crumpled.

Nick whirled his turret to follow the disaster. The leading Focke-Wulf staggered and fell into a hopeless spin.

"He hit the deck," Nick reported. "Blew up."

"That's one for you," Jesse said.

75

"Yeah, split about six ways."

"F . . fighter at twelve o'clock level." Eddie's mouth was bone dry, and the cold oxygen he gulped didn't help at all.

"It's a head-on," Jesse said.

"Show us how you got that prize at Tyndall field, Eddie."

The FW was huge in the gunsight, closing at a combined speed of more than six hundred. Eddie's fingers wouldn't behave, but the little dot in the middle of the sight reticle stayed steady on the German's spinner. The twin guns bucked. Eddie forced his fingers open. The burst had been far too long.

The fighter suddenly blew up—changing in an instant from an oncoming silhouette into a rolling ball of smoke. The B-24 bucked in the shock wave.

"What prize?" Terrible was saying as the clamor of Eddie's guns died.

"Doesn't matter," Morry said. "He just topped it."

Eddie didn't hear them. His body was convulsed with a frightening case of shakes. Was it always like this? He'd blown a man out of the sky with the first shots he'd fired for real. Was it always so easy?

"Can anybody see damage in the tail?" Jesse asked. "I think we were hit."

"Forward part of the left rudder," Hunky offered. "Looks like a shell went clean through."

The Focke-Wulfs got themselves better organized. A well-coordinated attack brought five of them screaming in from high above the rear of the formation, five more into each side, and three head-on. The bomber gunners fired furiously, turrets swiveling until the fighters broke off. In their wake, two B-24's drifted out of formation, one with two engines dead, the other showing no visible damage, but slowly

76

rolling to the left until it was knifing away at a right angle to the formation. Chutes began to bloom. One, then two at once, then another. Five . . . six. Half of them were out. The spiral tightened. The left wing folded gracefully, and the bomber was dead weight disappearing behind a distant hill.

Like crazed tigerfish, a swarm of fighters closed around the other crippled B-24. Silver shards flew from its engine nacelles. In less than a minute, it nosed down, fatally wounded, and sowed in its wake a neatly spaced trail of white parachutes, drifting like big dandelion seeds.

A single fighter barreled through the formation, its guns flashing at any target in sight. It came so close to Jesse's ship that every man inside could hear its peculiar high whine.

Now came the diving attacks, the FW's dropping on the bomber group like angry yellow-jackets, stinging hotly and with accuracy. They knifed down in little bunches of three or four until the whole squadron had sliced through the combat boxes. In their wake, the sky was criss-crossed with the smoke trails of dying B-24's. Scattered fires in the forests and fields along the bombers' flight path sent long black columns into the late morning sky. Three more Liberators had staggered out of formation and tumbled into the Yugoslavian mountains. Those remaining closed the formation and plowed ahead.

"Initial point coming up—now," Skinny reported.

The formation wheeled twenty degrees to the northeast and roared straight at its target. Directly ahead, at the intersection of the silvery Crna and Timok Rivers, lay Zajecar.

The fighters disappeared, but every man left in the air knew they hadn't pulled out for any reason other than to reload their deadly wing cannon.

Zajecar's flak guns opened up, dabbing the sky ahead with a tight group of black blots. "Well, they've sure improved," said Jesse.

The formation pushed into the flak field, bouncing across the concussions. A shell exploded a few yards above Jesse's ship, and Morry Flax ducked between the breeches of his guns. Not a fragment touched them. That's the "top-hat" pattern, Morry was thinking. Flak threw its shrapnel out in a circle and straight up in the center. If it burst above you, chances were good for a complete miss.

A shell crashed under their right wing. The ship rocked, and Morry came on the intercom with, "Hit us. Right wing tip full of holes."

Stav looked at Jesse anxiously. "Aileron damage?"

"Can't feel any."

The crew hunched deeper into their flak helmets and vests. Accurate flak was every bit as frightening as a careening fighter. You couldn't hit back. You sat in your aluminum eggshell and took whatever came.

But the flak field at Zajecar was mercifully short. The bombers got through with no apparent serious damage, and the target lay only a few miles ahead. If Intelligence had not determined that it was necessary to line up precisely along the axis of the valley, the Zajecar flak area could have been avoided altogether. The bomber formation shifted now, forming a train of elements that would lay their bombs on the target in a parade two miles long. With a renewal of fighter attacks likely, this was a highly risky maneuver. But a blanket bomb pattern by the much broader defensive combat formation would have had far less value against this target.

All bomb bay doors rumbled open. The bombardier in the lead ship of the first twelve-plane element hit his salvo toggle. The bomb string grew below his B-24. The others in the lead section dropped their bombs almost at the same instant, and the columns of black beads sank toward the mountains.

Jesse's element was over the valley now. Skinny Ennis rested his gloved fingers on the bomb release toggles. About a minute more . . .

He took his eyes off their flight's lead ship for an instant, stealing a glance through the heavy plastic panel in the floor just below Eddie's nose turret. In the valley, along the rail line, he spotted a brilliant pinpoint of light. Astonishingly, the light detached itself from the ground and rose rapidly toward them.

"Bombagator to pilot. Jesse, there's something odd down there—some sort of moving light."

"Drop, Skinny! The lead ship just let go, you're late."

Simultaneously, Skinny hit the bomb toggles and his mike button without taking his eyes off the mysterious light. "It's climbing, Jesse. I think it's coming straight at us."

The yellow-white pinpoint was growing larger; coming fast.

"Yeah, I see it, now." Jesse's voice was tense.

"I think it sees us, too," said Stav.

The thing had veered toward them.

"Do something!" urged Skinny.

"Like what?"

The light streaked upward relentlessly. Just before it hit, Skinny had a glimpse of a tapered nose, fins . . . In a second, the lead B-24 of Jesse's element erupted in a searing flash.

Far below, the bombs of the first wave marched their blast rings and smoke bursts along the west ridge of the deep valley.

"Everybody O.K.?" Jesse's voice was urgent.

Skinny struggled to his feet, the steel-plated canvas flak vest pulling heavily at his shoulders. He clapped his steel hat back over his flying helmet. "Bombagator O.K.," he gasped.

The rest of the crew checked in, their voices lacking their usual snap. Then Nick was back on the circuit.

"Another one. Coming out of the valley fast!"

They stared in horrified fascination. The second missile soared upward, correcting its course twice in abrupt swerves. An instant later, it bulleted into a B-24 far in the rear of the attacking column. The bomber disappeared in a second flash of fire.

A third missile rushed out of the valley and another Liberator was blown from the air. A thin smoke trail marked the missile's trajectory.

"Look sharp down there, Nick. I want to know the second you see any more of those things."

"What good is that, Jesse?" Stav said. "I think they've got themselves the ultimate weapon!"

"No good, maybe—but I can try."

Eddie's voice came on, struggling with words. "What . . . what is it?"

"Some kind of rocket. They've used them before, but not with guidance like this."

Now their own bombs were bursting directly below, marching along the valley slopes. A wide cloud of brownish smoke drifted across the target area.

The second element wheeled and followed the first element westward, heading home. No flak now; Zajecar was far to the south. But poised like angry hornets high above the reforming bomber combat box were the yellow-nosed

Focke-Wulfs of Kommando Boelcke, their fuel tanks full and their guns charged.

They hit hard, ten miles west of the target, chopping at the front and sides of the B-24 formation. A bomber sank out of position. Four Focke-Wulfs hacked at it as it floundered below fifteen thousand feet. Flame erupted from an engine, swept across the wing, and the B-24 plunged into a ponderous spin.

Another Liberator lurched away on an aimless course of its own. It sowed a line of parachutes in the frigid air, then nosed into a long flat dive that ended in the forest five miles below.

As the stricken bombers staggered out of formation, the remaining planes had tightened the combat boxes. Their screen of machine-gun fire remained unbroken. Few enemy fighters that struck at the desperately firing bombers got away unhit. But the FW-190 was a tough and heavily armored plane. After long minutes, one went down, its rudder shot away, the pilot rolling over the side just before his doomed fighter careened into a final looping dive.

Kommando Boelcke continued the ferocious attacks across sixty miles of central Yugoslavia. Another B-24 fell out of the squadron, trailing a thin black streak as the oil bled from one engine, and the second engine died of a severed fuel line. The hungry hornets bored in, and more parachutes drifted below the battle.

Then, with a suddenness that was entirely unexpected, the deadly Focke-Wulfs pulled off for the second time. The sky finally belonged to the ripped and battered Liberators.

This, Jesse realized, had been an expensive day. He had mentally tallied the planes that had gone down in the battle which had ranged across almost the entire breadth of Yugoslavia. The Luftwaffe had paid for their kills: two Messerschmitts, three FW-190's, and that mysterious little plane with no pilot.

But that price had bought plenty. Eleven B-24's, and the hundred men who had crewed them, would never return home. Eleven bombers had gone down—plus the P-51 near Bijelo Polje. That was a terrible loss, whatever the effects of the bombing mission. And Jesse had the disturbing idea that they had done very little damage to the installation northwest of Zajecar.

NINE

Although his china-smooth face was expressionless, Major Erwin Buckler was gripped by a rage that made the papers in his hands rustle, the only sound in his cramped office except his own angry breathing. It was midnight of a day that had been one long chain of confusion. And Erwin Buckler detested confusion.

First there had been the astounding arrival of the Reichsmarschall with his ridiculous visit to the old church. Then had come Buckler's helpless staring from the road along Rtanj Mountain as the American fighters chopped up eight of his Focke-Wulfs on the ground. They had also peppered the Reichsmarschall's plane so badly that a replacement had to be sent from Rumania to return Goering and his party to Berlin.

Then there was the matter of the target aircraft with its carefully installed radio and supercharger equipment. The idiots of the detachment from the factory had let it blunder into the bomber formation—with the inevitable result. They had made him look like six kinds of an incompetent, and he had fallen on them with a vengeance the moment Goering's party had boarded the Heinkel hurriedly summoned from Bucharest.

Of course, the day had had its compensations. Through Buckler's powerful binoculars, Goering had seen with his own eyes that the Klapperschlange was a remarkable success. Three missiles had streaked out of the distant valley, and three B-24's had simply disintegrated. And that, after all, was what Goering had come to witness. His elation, in fact, even canceled his stuttering anger at the fact that his personal plane had been strafed into uselessness before his eyes.

"There is no question, gentlemen," the Reichsmarschall had bubbled. "With this weapon and the others the Fuehrer has inspired—the V-1 and V-2—we will dictate terms before the snow falls on Berlin."

That, Buckler thought, was on the decidedly optimistic side. Still, the Klapperschlange had been amazingly effective. With a solid ring of them around every important target, Allied air power would be eliminated within months.

With or without the new weapon, Kommando Boelcke had done itself proud today. Eight of the fat B-24's had been sent crashing into the hills. The three Focke-Wulfs that had been lost were not too high a price to pay for eight bombers.

But the memory of Goering's face as the American Mustangs roared across the airfield below him set Buckler's nerves on edge all over again. He forced himself to concentrate on the reports he held before him now; reports on the

84

eight bombers his pilots had downed and the three that had been demolished by the Klapperschlange missiles.

None of them, apparently, was Number 401. Nearly thirty crew members who had parachuted from their falling B-24's had been captured by Wehrmacht patrols and sent by truck to Belgrade, where they were still undergoing interrogation. He planned to motor up tomorrow, although Stoltzman had argued against it. "No matter what Hauptmann Krafft has told you, major, we do not control the roads. The Partisans and Chetniks disappear as our patrols approach, and fifteen minutes later they are back."

"But I must question those men, nevertheless," Buckler said grimly.

"You have been given a full report by our people in the Foggia area," Stoltzman pointed out. "What more do you need?"

Buckler squinted at the papers in his hands. He had no idea how German intelligence worked such miracles, but here was a reply to his request of just a few weeks ago. The B-24 with the lightning slashes on its red fins and the serial number 401 belonged to the 747th squadron of the 456th bomb group based near Cerignola, Italy. Its pilot, the man Buckler determined to blast out of the sky—a determination which had sustained him through the black pain in the Berlin hospital—was named Stafford. An English name. The Americans were a strangely mixed race, and sometimes you could tell a lot by their names.

Stafford . . . he let his mind toy with that name. Small and crafty, no doubt. Dark. Little sunken eyes. Hawk-like eyes. A wiry man like a little Cockney. A snappish, crafty, little man. That would be Stafford.

Buckler forced his attention to another matter: replacements for the three planes he had lost, and two new pilots. One had returned, but the other two had not. He twisted the handle of his telephone. "Berlin," he ordered the operator. "Luftwaffe Headquarters."

Two minutes passed. He jiggled the receiver hook impatiently. "Corporal, my call, *bitte?* It is important. Have the Partisans found the wire to Belgrade again?"

"Nein, major. It is the lines into Berlin. Something is happening. There are too many calls, and they have clogged the circuits."

"Keep trying, corporal." A little chill of apprehension broke across Buckler's shoulders. In the past year, nothing really good had happened without the counterbalance of something not so good. "If necessary, I will try radio relay. And then courier, if I must."

Now that Goering had personally witnessed the success of the new weapon, Buckler was sure that, barring some sort of calamity, he could get from Berlin whatever he asked for.

He drummed his fingertips impatiently on the desk top, his mind returning again to the events of the afternoon. Goering had insisted that he be driven to the underground factory while they waited for the substitute plane from Bucharest. Buckler had been only too glad to oblige. He wanted to see it himself. They departed immediately after his group had landed, following their second attack on the B-24's. Stoltzman drove the open Mercedes with Buckler beside him. In the rear were Goering, Generaloberst von Schalluck, and Generalmajor Ebbing. Oberst Vogel had remained behind to complete the arrangements for the return to Berlin.

A quarter-kilometer from the underground complex, the roadway was cut by a wide bomb crater. They left the car and went on by foot. Around a sharp bend, the bombs had torn up a hundred meters of railroad track beside the road. The narrow valley still reeked of the fumes of high explosives.

In the three hours since the attack, the Wehrmacht work details had done a remarkable clean-up job. Damaged rails had been moved off the right-of-way, and salvaged ties were neatly stacked, awaiting the arrival of a work train from Zajecar. A small delegation of officers and civilian scientists appeared beyond another sharp twist in the canyon-like valley.

The introductions were stiff and nervous, the science people and installation officers suddenly acutely aware of just how important a group had walked into their valley. Hauptmann Ludwig Krafft, Buckler noticed with satisfaction, had turned as pale as celery.

They were given a royal tour. Buckler was fascinated by the entrance itself. The towering reinforced concrete door rolled sideways on hardened steel rails sunk in a protective trench. The rail spur from Zajecar passed straight through the eight-meter-high opening into a well-lighted interior. Scattered about the entrance were rock fragments from the shattering bomb detonations along the towering crests that formed a shield around the valley's dead-end. But there had been no hits on this part of the valley floor.

The interior workings were a strange combination of rough-walled natural grottos and precision machine tools, line after busy line of them extending far back into the mountain. With Krafft in the lead, Buckler's group visited the glassed-off research room, the fabrication chambers, assembly rooms, fuel storage area near the entrance, and the administration offices.

"And here," the neatly bearded scientist leading the tour

said triumphantly, "is the reason for all this." He slapped the big rocket that stood on its mobile launcher in the assembly room. "The weapon that will defeat the bombers. As you saw today. Small wonder we call it the Klapperschlange. The Rattlesnake."

The Klapperschlange lay in its steel frame launching cradle on a four-wheeled trailer. It was dull gray, torpedo-shaped, about four meters long with stubby wings and four large, square tail fins. Tubular booster units were mounted on the top and bottom of the main rocket. "Solid fuel units for instant ignition," their guide explained. "The liquid-fueled main motor ignites on the way to the target."

"And the guidance system?" Goering asked.

"A heat sensor, Reichsmarschall. The rocket homes in on the heat of a bomber's engines."

"The range?" asked Generaloberst von Schalluck.

"About ten thousand meters, we believe. You must understand, sir, that we are still in the testing stage with the rocket. The launching trailer is already proven. It can be stored anywhere; towed by any large vehicle. The cradle can be manually raised to firing position in three minutes."

Goering's eyes glittered. "With just a few thousand of these, gentlemen, I will eliminate the American Air Corps and the R.A.F. as effective bombing forces in two months' time. When can I have them?"

"Well, barring calamities, Reichsmarschall . . ."

"I will tolerate *no* calamities. I want them by midsummer."

"But that's impossible! We cannot—"

"We must, Doktor Arzt."

There had been a finality in Goering's words that unsettled Buckler. But it could help him, as well. With the Reichsmarschall's personal priority backing him up, Buckler knew he would be able to get replacement planes and pilots immediately. That made tonight's delay on the Berlin telephone trunk especially aggravating.

"I want you to keep trying, corporal," he snapped at his operator. "Notify me the instant you have a clear line, no matter what the hour."

The hour turned out to be twenty minutes after two in the morning. "I am very sorry for the delay, major. It was unavoidable."

"What do you mean, 'unavoidable'!" Buckler snapped. "I have tried to get through for more than three hours."

"It is the calls from the French coast," The Berlin military operator said. "There has been a sea and air bombardment. And now there are reports that parachutists are landing in Normandy."

Buckler hung the receiver on its wall hook, his mind racing with the impact of the Berlin operator's tumble of words. There would be no questioning of the captured Americans this morning. He would be too deeply involved in reorganization work. He knew now that no more replacement planes or pilots would ever come to his lonely airfield near Rtanj Mountain.

The news of D-Day brought changes to the 456th Bomb Group, as well. The B-24's began to range further north, deep into Austria. The emphasis was shifted from defending the Adriatic area to providing strategic support for the invasion of France.

But there remained the problem of the ominous weapon the Germans had used at Zajecar. Captain Edgar Tanner found himself concentrating with difficulty on the routine work of his intelligence section. He had studied the Zajecar mission strike photographs a dozen times. In the earliest photos, patterns of bomb bursts blanketed the target area at the end of the valley. In pictures taken later that day, after the smoke had drifted off the bombed area, there were no hits on the pinpoints; no hits on the factory entrance at all.

Tanner was not the only member of the 456th who felt this concern. In his tent at the far end of the officers' area, Jesse Stafford had spent hours flat on his cot, staring at the sloping tent above him, his mind seeing, not the faded khaki canvas, but that unbombable valley northwest of Zajecar.

There simply had to be an answer. And it wasn't another attack by heavy bombers, although Tanner had told him Wing was considering one. A strike by fast flying fighter-bombers? They couldn't carry bombs large enough to dent that entrance-way. The latest recon pictures had clearly shown a huge thick concrete doorway on heavy sunken tracks. "Reinforced just like the Saint Nazaire submarine pens," Tanner had confirmed.

"Suppose the fighter-bombers carried napalm?" Jesse had ventured.

"No good. Might warp the tracks a bit, if they managed to get it into the valley at all. But repair crews could replace them in a matter of hours."

"What then?"

"I don't know, frankly. You tell me, and I'll tell Wing. Somebody had better come up with something. I hate to think of a thousand or so of these deadly things around key targets. They'll make mincemeat out of us."

So Jesse forced himself to lie on his cot and just plain think; to let his imagination ramble; to search for a way to stop these accurate new rockets before they tore Allied bomber forces to tatters.

If there were only a way to steer a bomb once it was

dropped . . . by radio, perhaps. Radio! He thought of the pilotless plane that had blundered into the attacking bombers near Zajecar. A radio-controlled drone, the intelligence section had finally decided. Why it had been there remained a mystery.

Suddenly an idea found him, right out of the warm Italian noon.

Jesse scrambled off his cot so suddenly that Stav and Skinny stared at each other, mystified.

"What in the world bit you?"

But Jesse didn't even hear the question. He was already fifteen yards on his way to find Ed Tanner.

He tracked Tanner to the officers' mess, pulled him right out of the chow line, and half dragged him to an isolated empty table.

"This had better be good," warned Tanner. "Can't I even grab a cup of coffee to tide me over? I'll have to start at the end of the line again."

"You won't mind, I guarantee you." Jesse bent across the narrow table. "The only thing that will get that lousy concrete door is a big blast. Right? Something so heavy a bomber has to carry it, but something that can either drop straight down, or follow the bends of the valley. Well, we can't drop anything straight down, because of the bomber's forward speed. So we work on the other possibility."

Jesse's tone made Tanner forget all about lunch. "You've hit on something?"

"How about loading a war-weary with a full bomb load and flying it in there by radio?"

"Controlled from where?"

"From my ship, thirty-five thousand feet above the valley."

Tanner's eyes held Jesse's for almost half a minute. Then: "And what are the local Focke-Wulfs doing while you sit up there like a fat pigeon?"

"They're playing war games with a batch of Mustangs. This time, the Mustangs can wear their long-range fuei tanks all the way in. You told me that Messerschmitt group had been pulled out of Bileca."

"Right after the invasion. Goering's running short on his home grounds."

"We come up from the south at the same time the Mustangs hit them from the west. All the fighter boys have to do is keep them busy for half an hour."

"How do you know how long it would take to guide a B-17 into that valley?"

"I'm guessing." Jesse grinned. "You're way ahead of me, aren't you?"

"What do you mean?"

"You said a B-17. I didn't mention any particular plane."

"Well, that's the logical one. She's stable, maneuverable, a forgiving old girl. That's what you need. Not something tricky."

"Like a B-24?"

"You ought to know." Tanner hesitated a moment. "I wonder if one drone would be enough?"

"I just mentioned one because I know I'm going to volunteer."

"I'd rather you thought about, say, three."

"Why three?"

Tanner shrugged. "One's too few in case something goes wrong on the way to the target. Two are better. If you can get two, you can get three. Four are too many—that would be eight planes altogether. Too nice a group on a German radar screen. Suppose you could get authorization for three. Who else would you want?"

Jesse stood up. "I'll get you that coffee. You want milk and sugar?" He held the thick mugs under the urn spigot, his mind racing. When he returned and set Tanner's cup down, making a hot wet ring on the unpainted table, he said, "Marty Fields and Joe Carrone. They're good, steady, and I think they'd go for it."

"O.K. Here's what I'll do. Wing'll hear about this ridiculous idea within the hour. If you get authorization, you'll need some training. Probably somewhere nice and quiet where there aren't any interested field glasses around. That's nowhere in Italy I can think of."

"North Africa?"

"Probably."

"We'll need about three weeks to iron out the wrinkles after we get the B-17's."

"You'll have one week."

"One!"

"Oh, it won't be my decision. But I'll bet you any amount."

"And how long will it take to get the B-17's and the radio equipment?" Jesse asked.

"If Wing buys," Tanner said, sipping his coffee, "you can pack your bags tonight."

TEN

The mud-colored B-17 banked into its final approach, its engines quieting to a mutter. Its worn tires raced above the gravelly runway, then the bomber dropped in heavily.

"Fair," the instructor pilot said to Jesse. "You're still tense. Now give number three and four engines enough throttle to turn her."

The old Fortress lurched off the runway and taxied toward a little group of run-down stucco buildings a hundred yards off the cleared strip. The shell-scarred structures had once served as headquarters for a German fighter squadron assigned to General Erwin Rommel's Afrika Korps.

The B-17 lumbered across the rough taxi area. "Cut power," the instructor said, casually smoothing the little black moustache along his narrow upper lip. The four propellers windmilled to a stop, and the old plane seemed to

94

squat on the hard-baked desert, wanting only to be left alone.

And she was alone. Not a single crewman debarked. Not a helmeted face peered from her cockpit. Not a soul was aboard.

Jesse flicked off the switches of the transmitter control panel on the portable stand in front of the battered administration buildings. He straightened up and stretched.

A blanket of dry heat, a daily feature at this almost forgotten airfield, had already soaked the shirts of the three aircrews and their handful of support people. The detachment had arrived five days before by an Army transport ship which had docked at the North African port of Bengazi. From that Mediterranean city, they had journeyed by truck sixty miles eastward along the coast, then twenty miles inland to the isolated and deserted airfield.

The temporary training base consisted of the single runway of wind-swept "desert pavement." The cluster of chalky buildings was close by, and behind them was the scattering of brown tents the support staff had pitched. Along the west side of the runway were parked three B-24's: Jesse's Number 401 and the two assigned to Lieutenants Joe Carrone and Marty Fields. As Jesse had expected, both of them had been intrigued with the project. Near the B-24's were three old B-17's, Flying Fortresses, including the one Jesse had just landed by radio, their turrets removed and the holes covered with painted plywood.

Seen from the ground, the rust-colored desert flats stretched endlessly to the north, east, and west. Far to the south, low reddish hills shimmered in the heat. But when the B-24's rose on the thin air, the land to the north fell away rapidly and the crews could see the silver Mediterranean beyond the sun-scorched barrens. In all of Libya, only the areas around Tripoli and Bengazi were green. The rest of this hard land was a merciless desert, withered forever dry by the *gibleh*—the hot, dry breath of the Sahara.

"Brother! A week here is like six months anywhere else!" Nick Pastore grumbled as the large group of officers and enlisted men followed the instructor into the shade of the old stucco buildings.

"You volunteered like the rest of us," said Morry Flax. "It's better than getting shot at."

Nick kicked a stone, "That's still coming."

The crew members collapsed in the shadow of the ghostlike administration building, and the instructor pilot stood before them, hands in the pockets of his limp khakis.

"I've asked the enlisted crewmen as well as the officers to attend these sessions because I've always felt a crew works better when everyone on it knows just what's going on."

The instructor ambled to the bullet-chipped wall and leaned one shoulder against it. "All three of you pilots—" he nodded at Jesse, Marty, and Joe, who squatted together in a little group—"have really caught on fast to the radio control operation from the ground. Before we go into the airborne control work this afternoon, are there any questions on the project so far?"

"Yes, major," Joe Carrone said. He was a small stringy man from Baltimore's Little Italy. His side interest, Jesse had learned with surprise, was the gentle art of good cooking. "How much difference in control reaction can we expect when the drones are fully loaded for the mission?"

"The dummy loads in them now bring them up to almost three-quarters full load. There won't be much more lag. Just don't expect instant reaction on your switches."

"Major?" Marty Fields kind of bounced on his heels as

he talked. He was a smooth-faced blond; big, like Jesse, but boyish. He wore his bedraggled Dartmouth football sweater any time the temperature was below seventy. Today in Libya, it was closer to ninety-seven, and he wore a bleached khaki shirt with the sleeves rolled up.

"Yes, Fields?"

"How long before we're ready to try this crazy stunt?"

The major gave him an expressionless glance. "Forty-eight hours."

That gave them all something to think about, and Jesse suddenly felt as green as a spinach sprout; not sick-green, but fumble-fingered incompetent green. He'd been an idiot to push this lunatic scheme in the short training time available.

His performance that afternoon didn't make him feel any better. With Stav in the pilot's seat and a substitute co-pilot aboard, Jesse's B-24 swung back over the temporary field after a 1300-hour take-off. A thousand feet below, the pilotless B-17 had taxied into take-off position under the control of the instructor's ground set.

Crouching over the radio control equipment that had been installed in his Liberator's nose, Jesse wiped his palms on his flying suit. It was absurd to be this nervous, he told himself. But he couldn't shake the numb feeling that was exactly the same as that he'd had the day he made his first solo flight in a primary trainer.

"Control going over to you," the instructor's voice rattled in his earphones. "Now!"

Jesse switched on the control box between his knees. He advanced the four miniature throttles on the little console, and far below, the B-17's engines kicked up a cloud of tan dust. The distant Flying Fortress began to roll, veering to the left, and Jesse clamped the rudder switch to the right. The old Fortress angled back across the runway, gaining speed. Too much correction.

He tapped the rudder control lightly. The Fortress straightened its take-off run. Jesse eased the elevator control lever a touch forward. The tail of the war-weary Fortress lifted.

The throttles were full open now. The Fortress raced down the rough runway, trailing a long dust cloud. Jesse's forefinger edged back the elevator control. Far below, the Fortress slowly lifted free of its shadow. He thumbed a button, and a tiny bulb blinked out thirty seconds later to show that the drone's wheels had retracted into the inboard nacelles.

Without warning, the B-17's left wing dipped. The drone had flown through a thermal, a column of heated air bubbling up from the desert floor.

Jesse flicked the aileron control toggle. The drone righted itself sluggishly and rolled far to the right, its nose sinking dangerously.

Stav banked to pursue the erratic drone. Instinctively, Jesse's fingers followed the maneuver of the plane he was riding. The drone rolled almost vertical, slicing down, peeling off altitude.

With perspiration stinging his eyes, Jesse forced his entire attention to the runaway drone. He cut power, nudged the aileron toggle and eased back the elevator lever.

If he'd had any fingers free, he would have crossed them. The drone seemed bent on its own destruction. It raced toward its shadow, and Jesse already knew where the impact would be.

"Easy, now. Easy." The instructor's voice was distant. Jesse imagined him standing on his toes, helplessly watching the old B-17, tail high, plummet into the desert scrub, three miles from take-off.

The drone showed no sign of pulling out of its dive. Jesse had the elevator lever full back, but the nose still aimed straight at the ground. A feeling of angry frustration gripped Jesse. This was sheer murder, trying to fly a plane when you were nowhere near it.

Then a last frantic thought hit him. The B-17 wasn't simply in a dive; it had stalled out in the steep bank.

He shoved the two inboard engine controls forward. The distant propellers shimmered as their engines drank new fuel. The sudden slipstream drummed against the elevators, now full up.

Slowly, the big nose began to lift. The drone swept across the desert in a long arc, not a hundred feet over the ground at the lowest point, and climbed steadily into the open sky.

"Good show, Jesse," Stav said simply, but Jesse could sense an explosive gust of long-held breath from the other members of the crew.

In that instant of recovery, Jesse had reached the point that every good pilot must meet in learning to fly a new type of plane. It is a happy moment, because from that time on, the pilot feels that he, instead of the plane, is in charge.

During the next few training flights, the instructor knew that first Marty Fields, then Joe Carrone, had passed that crucial point. All three pilots were ready, now. The touchy business of loading the old Fortresses with tons of explosives began.

Under portable floodlights, ground crews and air crew members alike wrestled the bulky cardboard cartons of TNT blocks into the nose compartments, flight decks, waists, and tails of the worn-out B-17's.

"I didn't join the Army to be a pack mule," grunted Nick

Pastore, shoving a carton of explosive blocks into the nose of the drone assigned to Jesse's crew.

"Just keep working," growled Si-Si. "Everybody's a mule tonight. This is a low-budget operation."

Following the lashing down of the stacked cartons, five-hundred-pound general-purpose bombs were slowly hoisted into the bomb bays. Loading was completed at the flood-lighted hour of 0300. The crew members returned to their tents, and the steadier ones managed to get a few hours sleep. Nick Pastore's quiet snoring began the minute he stretched out in his sleeping bag. Eddie Jarman spent the hours trying to discover a comfortable position on the hard ground.

As dawn tinted the desert a harsh red, the rumble of twelve engines shook loose sand from the crumbling buildings near the runway. At short intervals, the three B-24's lunged down the runway and knifed into the cool morning air.

They wheeled in a loose circle west of the field. Now the ground personnel were ordered clear of the B-17 parking area. They double-timed a full mile and a half from the runway and took cover behind the low scrub.

A single man climbed cautiously into each loaded B-17. These were the arming officers carrying musette bags of fuses. In six minutes, their work was done. They boarded a jeep parked nearby, and they, too, left the area.

The radio control instructor, the only man remaining behind, hit the number one starter switch on the transmitter console. A hundred yards away, all four engines on the first B-17 began turning. Dust blossomed behind the tail. The drone taxied forward, swung to the right, and trundled to the head of the runway.

Five miles away, Jesse's B-24 pulled out of the holding

100

circle and approached the airfield. Crouching over his radio panel in the nose, Jesse took over from ground control. The Fortress began its take-off roll, the big white numeral One on its left wing gleaming in the newly-risen sun.

The two bombers climbed together, the drone a thousand feet below its mother ship. Behind them, Marty Fields picked up the second drone, and four minutes later Joe Carrone's B-24 guided the third into the air.

In less than an hour, the six planes had climbed high above the glittering Mediterranean Sea, the B-24's in a loose V two thousand feet above their drones. The old B-17's struggled for altitude, flying in a line abreast, a good five hundred yards separating their wingtips.

From a fisherman's boat on the placid water, the formation appeared to be a small squadron of half a dozen bombers on their way to Italy. But from the nose of Jesse's bomber, the flight was an exhausting struggle to keep a distant, heavily-loaded bomber in a straight climb, using only his fingers, which were already growing numb in his leather gloves. Drone Number 1 gently rose and sank well below and slightly ahead of its controlling B-24. It was the center B-17, flanked by Number 2 on the left—Marty Fields' drone—and Joe Carrone's Number 3 on the right.

The split formation passed well west of Crete at 0915. Three minutes later, Morry Flax sent a chill of alarm through the ship when he announced, "Bogies, eight o'clock high. About a dozen."

Gun turrets began to swing on the three B-24's. "Spitfires," said Terrible Cochran. "That's the fighter cover from Malta the R.A.F. promised as far as northern Greece."

They reached thirty thousand above a thin, milky undercast through which the sea could be seen only dimly. Another three thousand feet above the bombers, the Spitfires ranged back and forth, scanning the haze below them for any sign of an enemy fighter.

At this altitude, the bombers seemed to hang motionless in smooth space, their propellers apparently cutting a vacuum, their engines moaning with rhythmic monotony.

Jesse squinted through the heavy plastic observation window below Eddie Jarman's nose turret. Far to the east, a darker mass was visible against the slate-colored water beneath the haze.

Behind him, Skinny Ennis noticed his stare. "Peloponnesus," Skinny said. "The lower part of Greece. We're almost over the Ionian Sea."

Well clear of the Greek mainland, the planes of the compact bomber force droned north-northwest, their compasses aimed at the instep of the Italian boot, but their crew men occupied with thoughts of the opposite side of the Adriatic. What would it be like over the mainland with no fighter cover and three unwieldy, pilotless B-17's depending on them for every little control correction?

Forty-five minutes later, Stav's voice broke the silence of the intercom system. "Turning point coming up. Our friends are leaving."

The Spitfire formation passed a thousand feet overhead, the leader banking from side to side in a farewell salute, and faded to the south. In a shallow bank, the three B-24's changed course, their gyro compasses centering on a new heading: 045 degrees—northeast into the enemy mainland.

The same bright early summer weather that half-froze the crews of the three B-24's approaching northern Greece six miles high, made Erwin Buckler feel sticky, even though he had showered and pulled on a fresh uniform just a short while before. Or *was* it the weather? He paced back and

102

forth blackly behind the long line of alerted Focke-Wulfs. Where was the attack signal? Where?

He bit his lower lip, then stopped himself. Since he had been shot down, there had been no feeling in that lip. Not many days ago, he had bitten a deep cut in it without knowing what he had done until Stoltzman had told him he was bleeding. He remembered the incident well. It had been the moment that he had learned the Messerschmitt group was being pulled out of Bileca to be sent against Eisenhower's invasion forces.

Now Kommando Boelcke stood alone against whatever the Americans decided to throw against the Zajecar installation. He did not doubt for an instant that they would return, despite the terrible defeats they had suffered. You had to give the Americans credit, despite their hideous and vulnerable bomber designs. It was well-known throughout the Luftwaffe that fighters and flak had not yet succeeded in turning back a single American bomber attack. If any Luftwaffe pilot had thought otherwise, the battle of Schweinfurt last October proved the fact. Goering had thrown everything he had at the Eighth Air Force. The Americans had lost sixty planes and nearly seven hundred men, but they had hit the target anyway.

No, there was no hope that the Americans would forget Zajecar, Buckler thought grimly. And there was nothing on earth, he determined, that would stop his squadron from fighting them right down to the last Focke-Wulf.

Twenty minutes before, the message had come from the coastal early warning station at Dubrovnic that a force of P-51 fighters had crossed the Adriatic and was heading northeast. Was this the next move? Fighter-bombers? It wouldn't work. The entrance to the Klapperschlange factory was invulnerable to almost any bomb the Americans or the

103

R.A.F. could carry. Certainly no fighter could carry a bomb large enough to do any real damage at all.

But the Mustangs could reduce his defenses. They could chew up Kommando Boelcke until there was nothing left of it, and though they would then have to contend with the missiles, the rate of construction of those missiles was not rapid enough to hold off full bomber squadrons, let alone groups.

There was another point that concerned Major Buckler. Just a few days ago, on June 13th, Hitler had unleashed the V-1. The little winged, jet-engined bombs were buzzing into England from a hundred different launching sites across the channel. Buckler sensed a shift in interest from the experimental Klapperschlange to the operational V-1. It was ridiculous. The V-1's were being used willy-nilly against whole areas the size of London. The chances that they would hit something worthwhile were slim, indeed. But Hitler seemed convinced that the V-1's would so terrify the English that they would simply surrender. The Fuehrer should sit in a Luftwaffe fighter's cockpit over Sussex sometime, Buckler thought bitterly, and see just how the English felt about surrendering.

The klaxon horn on the airfield's radar trailer began its wild honking. From a dozen places, the fighter pilots dashed to their Focke-Wulfs. Buckler's ground chief helped him strap in, and up and down the line the big Junker Jumo engines began to growl.

The long-nosed fighters took off in groups of two and three as soon as they reached the downwind end of the strip. Their stork-legged landing gears folded neatly into the stubby wings, and Kommando Boelcke roared into the brilliant mid-morning sky.

Behind the impassive rubber and canvas of his oxygen

104

mask, Buckler struggled with a decision. Getting his planes into the air was an elementary move. Now they could not be strafed into uselessness. But now he had to make a more crucial choice: to fight or to wait? He could do both, but not well. Splitting the squadron into two elements would weaken both. Nevertheless, if he attacked the Mustangs with his full strength and they proved to be only a feint, he would leave the target exposed from some other direction.

"They are turning northward toward Belgrade," reported Buckler's ground radar control. "Wait. Wait. A small group has left the main force and is moving southeast toward you."

Ah, so he had been right. The large group was the feint. The actual attack would be made by the smaller flight. A clever plan, but their timing could have been better. Had they delayed only another few minutes, Buckler would have split his own force, sent half toward Belgrade and left half to patrol the Zajecar defense area. Now the inept timing of the attacking Mustangs had made his problem simpler. Let the Americans' main force go to Belgrade. Kommando Boelcke would wipe the sky clean of the smaller group of fighter-bombers that was now trying to sneak into the area from the north.

He gave the order, and the group howled upward, searching the cover of the sun. Forty thousand feet over the Danube, fifty miles north of Zajecar, Buckler spotted the enemy. There were twenty-four of them, their silver wings and fuselage little shining "T's" against the dark mountains. He signaled, and the full squadron arrowed down, angry hawks after unsuspecting field mice.

But the field mice had fangs. They dropped their long-range fuel tanks and scattered like a handful of paper, breaking their formation and turning tail for the northeast.

Buckler snorted. Green pilots. This wouldn't even be a challenge, this—what did the Americans call it? Turkey shoot.

The Focke-Wulfs streaked after the fleeing Mustangs, wheeling in a wide right turn and closing fast on their tails. A checker-board rudder passed across Buckler's flight path, and he pressed his electric cannon triggers. The four cannon drummed, vibrating the fuselage beneath him.

". . . to commander, come in, *bitte.*"

Although his guns had drowned the first part of the message, there was an unmistakable urgency in the radio call.

"Commander," he snapped in acknowledgment.

"Radar shows a small group of aircraft approaching from the south. Perhaps a half dozen. High."

"How high?"

"Ten thousand meters. Twenty-five kilometers distant."

Buckler was furious. "Within *twenty-five* kilometers before radar found them?"

"The mountains, major. They disrupt the transmission to the south—"

"Ja. Ja. Danke schoen, Control."

Now what? He had to revise his entire strategy right in the middle of a fight. Something else disturbed him, as well. These Mustang pilots were not green at all. One FW-190 already spun lazily out of the battle, trailing a fatal black plume. Clearly, the situation wasn't at all as he had believed it to be. He thumbed his radio button.

The shark-like Focke-Wulfs broke off the dog fight instantly and banked south, reforming as they pulled away from the Mustangs who seemed to have been caught flat-footed by the squadron's sudden pull-out.

If the newly-discovered planes on the radar screen were headed for Zajecar, the situation was already touch-and-go.

Buckler's FW's were more than twice as far from the mountain factory as were the newly-sighted planes.

He ordered full speed, and the screech of the big twelve-cylinder Jumos under forced draft echoed across the Morava Valley.

Halfway to Zajecar, Buckler finally realized that, like a mouse who thought he was more clever than the trap, he had been neatly outmaneuvered.

The main force of Mustangs had swung eastward from their Belgrade heading. Now, not ten kilometers directly in front of the rushing Focke-Wulfs, three dozen new Mustangs wheeled to meet Kommando Boelcke like a pack of hungry jackals. And a few kilometers to the north the original smaller flight of Mustangs—the very planes which had tempted Buckler into this trap—fast closed on his squadron from the rear.

Buckler had time for one quick moment of bitter admiration for the Americans' strategy. They were no doubt the most underestimated warriors in the world. Then the Mustangs dropped their wing tanks in a flurry of silver flashes, and bright orange began to dance along their wings.

ELEVEN

Si-Si Charles flipped his headset selector switch from "liaison" to "intercom." "Radio to pilot. I've picked up the German fighter frequency. They sound pretty excited."

"Right, radio. I've got our own fighter frequency on the command set. They've caught their pigeons." Stav clicked off, then came right back on. "All eyes, now, everybody. We're only twenty miles from target."

A quarter-mile off their left wing, Marty Fields had run into trouble. Sweat ran down his face and collected on his upper lip beneath his oxygen mask. His old B-17 drone had begun to have a mind of its own. It swerved to its right, shuddered under Marty's urgent control signaling, and swerved again.

"Blasted hunk of tin. I can't hold it straight. Something's wrong with the rudder control."

"You gotta hold it," said Marty's pilot simply. Like Stav, he was usually co-pilot of his crew, but in the left side of the cockpit now, he was in command of the bomber.

Number 2 drone veered sharply again. Marty toggled frantically, and the old bomber responded late and too little. It drifted away as if it were being pulled by an invisible elastic cord, struggling to return to Marty's guidance but powerless against the flaw in its control equipment.

In the lead B-24, Jesse stared as Marty's drone slid closer to his own. He hoped that Marty was just as alarmed. But he couldn't say a word to the other guidance pilot. They were under strict radio silence.

Stav's voice cut in loudly. "Isn't number 2 getting a little close?"

"Something's gone wrong over there. Looks like Marty's control is intermittent."

In clumsy lurches, the wobbling B-17 crept nearer.

"Good night!" shouted Jesse. "We're going to have a mid-air collision!"

Less than a thousand feet below him, Marty's drone closed on his own in a horrifying sideways drift that could only result in a blast that would blow them all out of the air.

"Dump it. *Dump it!*" Jesse's voice echoed along the intercom, and the other crewmembers were stunned to silence.

Just a few hundred feet separated the two drones. Jesse's fingers trembled on the control box. If Marty didn't—

The runaway B-17's nose sank. In a long curve, the drone fell away sharply and dropped far behind. Marty had sacrificed.

His drone, now completely beyond control, plunged into a screeching spiral, whirled through twenty-five thousand feet of summer sky and slammed into a mountainside at four hundred miles an hour.

At thirty thousand feet, the sound of the impact was lost in the formation's roar, but the huge concussion ring was awesome. It spread from the orange explosion in a gigantic widening doughnut, ripping leaves from the trees in a vast circle. A fountain of dirty brown and white smoke spouted upward, detached itself from the ground and rose eastward, an awesome shapeless balloon following its shadow across the mountains.

Obeying the pre-take-off instructions, Marty's B-24 stayed in the loose formation. The other two bombers would need his guns if the Focke-Wulfs managed to break past the Mustangs.

Zajecar drifted past them, to the east. The town's few flak guns reached out ineffectively, their shells bursting almost two miles from the bombers.

The narrow valley leading to the target was visible now, a thin ravine twisting northward through the rising blue mountains.

Two hundred yards to the right of Jesse's bomber, Joe Carrone's fingers nudged the controls of his drone. It nosed down slightly and grew smaller.

Jesse guided his own B-17 in lazy left and right yaws, giving Carrone's bomber time to pull well ahead. Then he straightened the drone's flight path deftly, dropped its nose, and followed the other B-17's flat dive.

Six miles below, Hauptmann Ludwig Krafft was resisting the temptation to run in helpless circles. The attack warning from the airfield radar van had come in long ago by telephone. Buckler and all his pilots had disappeared to the northeast. Krafft felt deserted, although he had gloated only the day before to Buckler that the Klapperschlange would soon make the Luftwaffe unnecessary.

110

That had been big talk, but Krafft honestly believed it. There were a few kinks, of course, to be ironed out. One of them was the problem of fueling the main motor. Nitric acid and sulfuric acid were not the easiest fuels to handle. Goering had been told that the Klapperschlange could be readied for firing in three minutes, but the chief scientist hadn't pointed out that the three minutes began after the fuel for the main motor was piped in.

Now Krafft paced the stone floor of the cavern's flight preparation room, tempted to shout at the smock-clad technicians bustling about the five rockets on their train of flat car launchers.

The incredible fools! Did they dare pretend that this weapon with its agonizing fueling time would even get into a battle, let alone win one?

One of his helmeted Wehrmacht guards signaled him to a wall phone. "Observation Post Two, Herr Hauptmann," a distant voice scratched. "There are five bombers approaching from south-southwest."

Bombers from the south? He had expected fighters from the opposite direction, according to what he had been told by Kommando Boelcke's radar unit.

"How far distant?"

"Eighteen kilometers, sir."

"That close? What is wrong with the radar to permit them to come so close undetected?"

"The mountain, Herr Hauptmann—"

Of course. Rtanj Mountain blocked the radar transmission southwards. He felt a cold premonition. He clapped the phone back on its wall hook and trotted to the rocket train.

"Open the doors and get these things outside."

The chief technician, a lumpy-faced civilian with tiny eyes, glared at him. "Only two of them are fueled. We will be ready in fifteen minutes."

111

"You idiot! There are five bombers not five minutes away." Krafft's face reddened to a ripe beet color, and the technician swallowed hard.

"You will detach the three unfueled rockets immediately and move the other two into firing position."

"But, Herr Hauptmann—"

Krafft unbuttoned the flap of his pistol holster. "Do you want to lose the war right on this spot, *unwissend Schwein?*"

The civilian gave a rapid string of orders to his crew. The two self-propelled flat cars rumbled along their tracks as the floor vibrated with the opening of the main portal.

It was always an impressive sight, this rolling back of tons of steel and concrete to reveal the harsh walls of the valley beyond. The two flat cars trundled through the opening, their rockets already elevating into position. The mighty door rolled shut with an echoing clang, and Krafft stepped into a tiny elevator off the fueling room.

He emerged high above into a beautifully camouflaged bunker, nodded at the four observers on duty, and stepped into the sunshine. The observation bunker crouched on the brow of the hill overlooking the end of the valley. The cliff fell steeply below Krafft's feet, a sheer one-hundred-meter vertical face. At its base, the huge factory door looked tiny from this height. The tracks emerging beneath it were parallel pencil lines along the valley's shadowed floor. They snaked out of sight around the first bend, a quarter kilometer distant. Between the factory entrance and the bend, the two Klapperschlange anti-aircraft rockets nosed skyward on their launching cars, waiting and eager. The two firing technicians had strung out their ignition cables and had taken cover beyond the bend.

Krafft shaded his eyes and peered south. He could hear them now. A distant rumble.

"Glasses, Herr Hauptmann."

He took the binoculars from the bunker sergeant and adjusted the lenses. There they were, but it was a strange formation. Three bombers were grouped high together, while two more sank rapidly, growing larger as they picked up speed.

A chill made the binoculars shake in Krafft's chunky fingers, and that surprised him. He had been in battle along the Russian front and had never known real fear. But something about the two diving bombers made his stomach twist.

Strafers? No. Sending bombers to strafe the valley would be useless, and the Americans must realize that. Something far worse than machine guns was screeching into his canyon.

He glanced downward at the waiting ground-to-air rockets. Fire, you fools. Fire!

As if its operator had heard Krafft's unspoken plea, the first Klapperschlange kicked out a fiery skirt of flame and smoke. Its roar hit Krafft with a solid wall of sound.

The sergeant tapped his arm and brought his mouth close to Krafft's ear. "We must get into the bunker, sir."

With its booster tubes spitting frothy white plumes, the rocket leaped out of the valley. At a thousand meters, it veered sharply southward, still climbing rapidly.

"Herr Hauptmann," the sergeant persisted.

Krafft shook his arm free, his eyes glued on the bright tail of the rocket. The exhausted booster motors flew off and tumbled out of sight beyond a distant mountain crest.

The oncoming bomber didn't change its course by even a degree. The Klapperschlange arrowed into it a full three kilometers from Krafft's hilltop, but the effect was astounding.

For an instant, the entire sky seemed ablaze with brilliant

yellow-white light that seared Krafft's eyes. He drew back instinctively and threw his arm across his face. The shock hit him in a huge invisible wave of force. He was punched completely off his feet and flew backwards to tumble face up among the scrubby weeds of the hilltop.

He struggled for breath, hanging limply in the arms of the bunker sergeant who had dashed to him after the shock wave rolled beyond them.

Half dragged into the bunker, Krafft shook the sergeant's supporting arm free and stumbled to the forward observation slit. A great rolling ball of smoke drifted eastward from the far end of the valley. Beyond it, the second low-flying bomber grew larger in its long dive. Below him, out of view through the narrow observation port, and over the ringing in both ears, Krafft heard the rumble of the second Klapperschlange.

In the frigid sky south of the target, Jesse had grunted in despair when Carrone's drone had been blown to bits by what appeared to be one of the same weapons used against the bombing attack a couple of weeks ago. Now only Jesse's drone remained.

He eased back the elevator toggle. The radio-controlled bomber flattened its dive until it was skirting the mountains near the valley mouth. His plan was to skim the B-17 straight along the hill crests until it was almost on top of the factory entrance. Then he would cut power completely and dump the nose full down. The tree-top approach should protect the drone against all but small arms fire from the ground. But if they launched another of those rocket things. . . .

The very instant the thought crossed Jesse's mind, another rocket streaked out of the deep defile, etching a white trail across the blue mountains.

It rose perhaps three thousand feet, then wavered uncertainly and bore down on the drone. Jesse smiled tightly behind his oxygen mask. The missile was confused. It had begun an upward trajectory. Then suddenly its sensors had found the low-flying B-17 and revised the original course.

Jesse advanced the engine controls to full open and banked the old B-17 sharply left. The plume of white cut off abruptly as the solid fuel boosters broke free of the missile. Now it was only a bright flame streaking across the hills.

Jesse's gloved fingers flicked across the control console. The drone kicked its left wing high and swung to the right.

The rocket veered, but the combination of its own abrupt flight path change and a rapidly-shifting target was too much for its guidance system. It slammed into the rocky ground a quarter-mile behind the drone, the explosion an orange-centered gray puff from thirty-thousand feet.

Missed me! Jesse realized triumphantly. But his elation was cut short when the old B-17 slewed wide on his turn recovery signal, and skidded eastward. Desperately, he toggled left turn signals. The drone slewed around and once again headed for the target. But now it approached from the east; not up the valley, but across it.

Jesse made a tough decision. "I can't drop it in over that high ridge on the east side. I've got to circle the drone around to the left and bring it up the valley again."

That meant more long exposed minutes for the three B-24's. He wouldn't blame Stav if he told Jesse to drop the drone as near the target as he could and forget another run. But Stav was as much of a professional as Jesse. "Go ahead with a second run, Jess. We'll make a wide swing around the target to the east. That ought to give you time."

"I can't see what's going on up there," Terrible Cochran said from his tail turret, "but I sure hope those Mustangs can keep those Focke-Wulfs occupied."

The Mustangs were, in fact, doing a beautiful job, as Erwin Buckler would have been the first to agree. Trapped between their two formations, Kommando Boelcke was fighting for its life. Three Focke-Wulfs had already spun into the hills, hanging blue-black streaks in the clear air behind them. A Mustang shed its left wing, and the white disc of a parachute followed it into a distant canyon.

Not until his ground controller came on the air again did Buckler realize that even this elaborate fighter trap was itself a diversion for yet another objective.

"Bombers are attacking *Der Berg,*" the controller announced, using the code term for the underground factory.

"How many from what direction?"

"Not more than a half-dozen. From the south. One has been shot down. Another is circling for a low level attack."

Low level? That didn't sound right at all. Six bombers coming in at low level? The control column vibrated in his hand, and from the corner of his eye he saw pieces flick from his right wing tip. Buckler booted left rudder and dropped the lean nose in a steep power spiral. High above him, the attacking Mustang's guns bit at thin air.

Only six bombers? He signaled Oberleutnant Pichler, and Pichler's group of twelve fighters broke off the fight and sped south behind Buckler. It had been a question of leaving the rest of the squadron to face even higher odds against the eager Mustangs, or letting the bombers have their way. Buckler's assignment was protection of The Project. He had done what he had to, and he tried not to think of the massacre that could take place, now that he had pulled Pichler's group out of the fight.

Four minutes later, he couldn't believe his eyes. A single bomber—a B-17—was circling the target area at less than two hundred meters. But fighter control had said six bombers were in the area. He swept the sky methodically. There, at perhaps ten thousand meters, were three B-24's. Buckler was puzzled. They were flying westward, north of the target. This didn't make sense. He could see no smoke rising from bombs already dropped, only a blue-brown smudge drifting away far to the east.

The B-17 was swinging into the lower end of the valley. Buckler thumbed his radio button. "Pichler, attack the B-24's. I will deal with that idiot in the B-17."

He peeled off, right wing high, and screeched down an invisible ramp of turbulent air. The Fortress wobbled along the valley, banking sluggishly to line up on the underground factory five kilometers distant. Buckler came in high from the tail. The B-17 grew in his gunsight. He braced himself for the expected streams of tracers from the top and tail turrets, but they never came.

His fighter bounced under the recoil of its cannon. The B-17's left wing lost its tip. Buckler held the firing button down and touched right rudder. The yellow flashes of exploding shells danced inboard across the left engines. A propeller lost its shimmer and windmilled uselessly.

No answering guns. The realization hit home. Something was wrong here. It was as if the bomber had no one alive aboard, or no one aboard at all.

The B-17 tilted fatally, and Buckler was clutched with instinctive fear. He rammed his throttle full forward, hauled back the stubby control column, and the Focke-Wulf leaped high over the valley.

He was nearly three kilometers distant when the Fortress skipped across a rocky knob, left a wing skittering along the ridge, and plunged into a narrow defile near the main valley.

The concussion threw the fleeing Focke-Wulf into a shuddering nose-high stall. Buckler dumped the stick, and rode a rolling washboard downward, fighting for airspeed.

He pulled out three hundred meters above the mountain crests. Incredible! The bomber had obviously been crammed with explosives for a ramming attack on the target. But Americans weren't the type to order suicide missions. Even volunteers wouldn't be accepted. There couldn't have been anyone aboard. He pondered a moment, then he knew. Of course. The B-24's. Mother ships. Buckler scanned the sky to the west. Pichler would take care of them.

But Pichler didn't even come close. Craning his neck to the rear, he had seen the astounding explosion that followed Buckler's attack on the lone B-17. Even at this distance he and his pilots felt the fist of concussion.

They climbed at full throttle despite the warning of their fuel gauges. But the B-24's had streaked west the instant the other bomber had crashed. They had the advantage of altitude, and apparently their bomb bays were empty.

Pichler knew their airspeed at ten thousand meters was more than three quarters that of his Focke-Wulfs. He could catch them eventually, of course, but there would be no fuel left for battle. Reluctantly, he radioed his pilots and they turned back, blaming themselves for a bitter morning over which they had actually had very little control.

What disturbed Pichler most was his commander's insistence on what seemed to be a very minor point. "But you must have gotten closer, oberleutnant," Buckler persisted. "You must have at least seen their numbers. Tell me, Pichler, could not one of them have been number 401?"

"I don't know, major. I swear we did not—"

"But it could have been, could it not?" Buckler's mask of a face was blank, but his eyes were pleading.

"*Ja,* major. One of them could have been, of course." Pichler was glad to get out of the office.

118

TWELVE

Goering's voice at the Berlin end of the phone was elated. *"Wunderbar,* major! You have done an excellent job. You say there were two of the radio-controlled bombers?"

"Three, Reichsmarschall. We found one later about twenty kilometers to the south. It must have crashed en route."

"Well, you did an excellent job today."

Buckler bristled then fought control of his temper. *"Nein,* Reichsmarschall. We were lucky. But our luck didn't cover our losses. What I need desperately are more fighter planes."

There was a long silence. Then, quietly, Goering said, "Impossible, I regret to say. Have you any idea what is going on in France and on the Eastern front?"

Buckler knew better than to attempt an answer.

"There are no planes to spare, major." Goering went on.

119

"The Fuehrer has ordered all fighter production shipped immediately from final assembly to the active fronts."

"But, Reichsmarschall, this, too, is an active front. The Russians are reported to be massing supplies along the Rumanian border even now."

"I can supply ammunition and fuel," Goering said, as if he hadn't heard Buckler's protest, "but you will have to succeed with your present aircraft. Good hunting, major."

Buckler pounded his desk in silent fury. He now had few more than forty airworthy planes to challenge an enemy who had begun to use ingenuity that Buckler hadn't remotely expected. "Good hunting," indeed! That was like wishing the fox good hunting at the moment the hounds were let loose.

Wearily, he reached for the telephone once again. "No more shifts," he ordered the maintenance chief. "Your men must work until they cannot continue, then they may rest four hours only."

The maintenance chief grunted as if he had been struck in the stomach, but all he said was, *"Ja,* Herr Major," in a dull tone.

In an attempt to inspire him a little, Buckler added, "It is a personal request of Reichsmarschall Goering."

"Ja, Herr Major," the other voice repeated flatly. If he'd said, *"Vive la France!"* Buckler couldn't have disciplined him with a clear conscience. He had just asked for more than he knew his men could give.

Buckler folded his arms and stared at an identification silhouette pinned above his desk. The Americans had played a clever hand today, and although it hadn't won the game, their attack had revealed something that made Buckler shift uneasily in his chair. Would the Americans realize it?

"I would suspect," Captain Edgar Tanner was saying at that very hour at 456th Intelligence Headquarters, "that the defending squadron is in a real bind."

"They're not the only ones," Jesse put in.

"What're you complaining about? You didn't even get seriously shot at today."

"Didn't hit the target, either. The whole plan was ridiculous. I risked three crews for nothing."

Tanner took off his glasses and polished them with the end of his khaki tie. He had just come from a meeting at Wing, and his uniform was neatly pressed, in contrast with Jesse's rumpled suntan shirt and trousers.

"I wouldn't say you flew that mission for nothing," the intelligence captain said slowly. "Your basic idea was completely sound, but there are too many parts in a B-17. Too many things to go wrong. And those old war-wearies we gave you were one step from the elephants' graveyard."

Jesse studied him. "You're leading up to something, aren't you?"

"Yes, I am. That's why I asked you to come over here to the intelligence section tonight. They're pretty excited about your remote control idea up at Wing."

"I'll bet they are. Three misses."

"Well, I'll grant you they'd rather be discussing hits. But something's come up. Or rather, it's been up for a while, but nobody's been interested in trying it before."

"What are you talking about, Edgar?" said Jesse impatiently.

Tanner replaced his glasses, seating them carefully on the bridge of his thin nose with a thumb and forefinger. "It's called the Azon—a two-thousand-pound general-purpose bomb that can be radio controlled in azimuth. Left and right."

Jesse forgot how tired he was. "A bomb you can guide to the target?"

"Something you once suggested yourself."

"But I was kidding."

"Well, somebody else wasn't. They've been working on it for some time, I understand. You still need a bombardier because it has to be dropped the right distance from the target, like a regular bomb. But after it's launched, the Azon can be steered right or left into the target."

"When can we get our hands on those things?"

Tanner smiled. "I've been pulling a string or two since I heard about them. How many do you want?"

"You mean they're that available?"

"You come up with a plan," Tanner challenged, "and Wing will come up with the Azons. And that's straight from General Thiebold, himself."

Jesse pushed himself away from the door jamb where he had slouched, hands in his pockets, and strode across the small office to perch his two hundred pounds on Tanner's desk. "All right, genius. Tell me everything you know about the Azon."

That took an hour. And in another hour, Jesse had worked out a battle plan he insisted Tanner take right back to Wing for approval.

"You mind if I go through channels?" Tanner suggested. "After all, you do work for the 456th, you know."

"Check with anybody you have to, but get approval."

Tanner slapped on his battered garrison cap and headed for the door. "You know," he said, turning back in mid-stride, "your crew won't like this idea much."

"They don't have to like it. They'll do it because they're a good crew."

Jesse knew his men well. Twenty-four hours later, after

he had told them of Wing's approval for his plan, Morry Flax summed it up neatly. "I don't like flying with a different crew any more than the rest of you, but I like that cruddy target even less. If this trip'll do the job, I'll even go there on a Greyhound bus."

Nick Pastore bent over the oil drum that served as a makeshift stove in the center of the six-man tent and sniffed the bubbling coffee pot. "You gotta admit, it's going to be a weirdo mission."

"Like that last one," Terrible Cochran put in.

"Worse. You and Hunky are going to be on a B-24 missing eight of its ten guns. You guys can have it. I'll gladly take the assignment I drew."

"That's a little strange, too," Hunky Molnar pointed out. "Who ever heard of a *P*-24?"

They all realized that if destruction of the target near Zajecar wasn't considered absolutely essential, Wing would never have even considered Jesse's unprecedented scheme. It called for more than shuffling crews. The plan also required the modification of three bombers: Joe Carrone's, Marty Fields', and Jesse's own, Number 401.

The work took almost a week. In that time, a trio of USAAF cargo planes had quietly flown seventeen Azon bombs from their assembly plant in the western United States to North Africa. They landed in the rising noon heat at the old Luftwaffe base so familiar to the three crews due in the next day. A cadre of ground personnel manhandled the unfamiliar cargo into sandbagged bunkers a half mile from their temporary camp. "Funny-looking bombs," a corporal decided. "The fins are so big."

A nearby sergeant growled at him, "You ain't supposed to be a commentator, Harrigan. Leave that to Edward R. Murrow and just shove, will ya?"

The following day brought heat, dry desert wind, and the three Liberators from the 456th Bomb Group. For a few minutes after they landed, they got little attention. The crews debarked and carried their duffel bags to the tents they had been assigned.

Back on the line, a mechanic ambled over to his crew chief. "What're you starin' at, sarge?"

"You ever see anything like that?"

The mechanic squinted at Jesse's Liberator. "Now that you mention it, what happened to her turrets?"

"Stripped off. All of them. That greenhouse nose must've come from an old B-24D, and the tail windows look like a home-made job."

"You think one gun in the nose and one in the tail is enough? That's only two guns instead of ten."

"You see those other two ships?"

The mechanic ambled down the line to the two Liberators flown in by Marty Fields and Joe Carrone. He let out a low whistle. "That's somethin', chief. Six extra guns apiece! They're flying battleships."

Both B-24's had been modified the same way. An opening had been cut behind the upper turrets, and dual hand-held machine guns protruded from the cramped space above the bomb bays. Another set of hand-held caliber fifties stuck out of the bottom of each bomber, aft of the rear hatchway. And two guns jutted from each waist window, instead of the customary single barrel.

"What do you make of all that?" the mechanic said.

"I don't know. But I'd guess they're trying to make tigers out of those elephants."

The air crews and the little group of civilian instructors met at the rear of the old administration building as the red sunset faded into a cool, dry evening. A thrumming gen-

124

erator provided the electricity for the bare electric bulbs strung across the battered stucco wall.

Jesse was the first speaker. "You've all been told why we're here, but I'm going to remind you once again. Knocking out that factory near Zajecar can save I don't know how many bombers and their crews. You've seen what those missiles can do."

He thrust his hands in his pockets and ambled along the front row of squatting airmen. "This isn't going to be a repeat of our last trip. That was one whale of a good try by all of you, but what we had to work with just wasn't good enough. This time, I think we've got what it takes."

He searched out his own crew in the dim glow of the wavering bulbs. "Some of you will be flying with other crews. I know that's always a hard thing to do, but you're here because you're top people. You do what has to be done, and you do it well. My ball turret and nose turret gunners will fly on Lieutenant Carrone's ship as auxiliary top and belly gunners. My top turret gunner and my radioman will handle the extra gun positions on Lieutenant Fields' plane. I'll be just as proud of their work as if they were on my own bomber.

"Now I want to introduce Dr. Roger Thurmont, an electronics engineer who has been sent along with the Azons to show us how they work. I want all of you to pay strict attention now. I know Dr. Thurmont doesn't wear bars or stars on his shoulders, but as far as I'm concerned, he's the general here. We do what he tells us until we're headed toward Zajecar three days from now. Doctor, you can have the floor."

Jesse sat down with the rest of the officers and men as the chunky bald-headed engineer walked to the front of the group. He wore a khaki shirt and trousers and had a large

125

red bandanna around his neck. The shiny dome of his scalp reflected the gleam of the generator-fed lights as he faced his audience and fiddled with a little black tubular device.

"This," he began abruptly, holding the little tube up for them to see, "is an item that must remain nameless. But it is the heart of the Azon guidance system. It's in the tail of each bomb, and it translates the guidance impulse into a fin movement, thus steering the bomb. That's all you have to know about the inner workings, gentlemen."

He stuck the electronic tube in a hip pocket and folded his arms. "There are seventeen Azons on those carts over there beyond the tents. First, there will be three practice drops for each crew. That, including the installation of a guidance transmitter in each plane, will take up two days. On the third day, we will load two Azons in Lieutenant Carrone's plane and two in Lieutenant Fields' plane. The third plane, flown by Lieutenant Stafford, will carry four Azons."

His eyes swept along the rows of crewmen. "These bombs weigh two thousand pounds each. That will mean eight thousand pounds in Lieutenant Stafford's plane. That's why the turrets have been removed. The plane has been stripped of all excess weight. Much of the radio equipment has been taken out, as well. To make up for the loss of firepower, the lieutenant tells me the other two planes have been supplied with extra guns."

He cleared his throat. "Well, now, to get on with the technical side of it, the Azon is officially known as the VB-Two . . ." He warmed to the subject he knew best, and the briefing lasted another hour. When it broke up around 1700, Nick Pastore stretched noisily.

"I feel like I've been briefed for a mission, gone to elec-

126

tronics school, and had a course in armament—all in one sitting."

"We have," Morry Flax said dryly. "Let's hope this is the last time we have to hit Zajecar. I don't think I can handle any more technical training."

By late afternoon the next day, the three B-24's were in tight formation twenty thousand feet above the desert. To the south, the rugged mountain ridge of Al Jabal thrust its rocky shoulders into the dancing heat waves. On the twenty-mile-wide apron of level sand and gravel between the saw-toothed mountains and the Mediterranean's slate-like glitter lay a tiny cluster of five abandoned Afrika Korps half-tracks. "Your target, gentlemen," the squint-eyed chief civilian instructor had said before take-off.

He crouched beside Skinny Ennis, studying every move the bombagator made. Skinny was glued to the eyepiece of his bombsight, carefully lining up the horizontal cross hair, but purposely neglecting the vertical.

"You must drop the bomb the proper distance from the target, but you needn't be in line with the target," the instructor had cautioned.

"Ten seconds to 'bomb away'," Skinny announced.

The distant desert junk drifted across the bombsight's field of vision toward the horizontal cross hair. Skinny's thumb found the release button. The B-24 lifted and Jesse leveled her instinctively. "Bomb away," Skinny announced.

The Azon dwindled below the observation panel in the floor of the nose. A thin stream of smoke trailed behind the chubby bomb, then a bright light bloomed in the tail fins.

"That's the high intensity flare," the instructor barked into the intercom. "You can follow the bomb visually all the way down. Try a left turn, Ennis."

127

Skinny flicked the radio control switch on the little black metal console beside the bomb sight. The Azon skidded and veered five degrees left.

"Now to the right."

He flipped the control again. The bomb, only a glowing pinpoint of light by now, veered into a new path.

"O.K. You're getting down there now. Let's see you hit the target."

Skinny eyed the little group of dots in the sand and touched the control level. The white light seemed to be skimming along the ground now, an optical illusion familiar to all bomber crews. The light veered toward the target.

A mile or so to go. Skinny could see that he was going to miss by a good five hundred feet. He tapped the switch angrily, and tapped it again. The light lurched twice, fell into the groove he wanted, and smacked dead center among the old vehicles. A snow-white puff of marker smoke spurted above the target and drifted eastward after its shadow.

The intercom was alive with gleeful congratulations, and a grin spread across Skinny's face. This, he decided, was really going to be something.

THIRTEEN

Erwin Buckler joggled the telephone receiver cradle impatiently. Now even basic communications were in a mess. It was the fighter-bomber raids. Since the bomber drone attack, Mustangs and P-38 Lightnings from Italian bases had begun daily strafing runs on Buckler's airfield. The attacks were at different hours, perhaps one at dawn, then another at sunset.

Seven days ago, they had come twice. Eight twin-tailed Lightnings snarled in exactly at noon, only three minutes after Buckler had managed to get his planes airborne. When they had gone, after a brief dogfight in which neither side lost an aircraft, the P-38's fled westward and Kommando Boelcke returned to the foot of Rtanj Mountain. All but two Focke-Wulfs had landed when a dozen Mustangs screeched out of the sun and laced the field from one end to the other with fragmentation bombs.

The squadron had lost ten planes. A day later, two more were shot down by a force of fifteen Mustangs that had roared around Rtanj Mountain, low enough to shake the leaves on the slopes, and had caught them taking off. The Americans lost three in the dogfight that followed, but Buckler knew their P-51's would be shortly replaced. His two Focke-Wulfs were gone forever.

He was forced to disperse his remaining two dozen FW-190's. He and his three commanders scoured the countryside by automobile and found almost a dozen pastures and farm fields good enough for minimum take-offs and landings. Two or three of the long-nosed fighters were flown to each field and hidden in among the trees or in nearby barns and sheds. At the fighter base, Buckler ordered his mechanics to build dummy planes from the hopeless wrecks that had been collected at one end of the field. Then the ground crews began their endless rounds of servicing the more than twenty fighters hidden various distances from the main field.

The American fighter planes apparently had not connected the old monastery with the fighter operations. Since it remained untouched Buckler kept his headquarters where it was.

Without proper telephone communication, he felt isolated and helpless. His pilots had congratulated him on his idea of dispersing their planes, but he knew that the measure was strictly a stop-gap. How could two dozen battered Luftwaffe fighters hold off an entire air force? That, he felt, was what the Americans would use if they had to. Now he fully understood Rommel's remark when he learned that Americans had landed in North Africa. One of his officers, went the story, had asked the general what he thought of the Americans' fighting ability. "It makes no difference," the Desert Fox was supposed to have snapped. "Once

130

Americans get a foothold, they simply drown you in supplies."

Buckler had read the Berlin reports on the thousand-plane raids over Germany, and his mask-like face had twisted into his closest imitation of a bitter smile. All the 15th Air Force had to do, he thought, was send a thousand bombers to Zajecar, their bomb bays filled with dirt. They could simply fill up the valley. A moment later, he decided that wasn't so funny, after all. The Americans had probably thought of it themselves, chuckling as they went on to a more threatening plan.

What would it be this time? What did it matter, actually? He would fly and fight until there was nothing and nobody left to fight with, and that would be that. Until then, he would get the telephone line repaired if he had to climb the poles himself. He fought the impulse to rip the whole thing off the wall and throw it in the trash basket, when it clicked twice and Krafft was on the line.

"*Ja, Ja,* major. What is it?" Krafft's voice was impatient, almost angry.

"Simply the daily status report."

"Well, the status is the same as yesterday."

"No progress, then."

"Certainly progress," Krafft snapped. "I told you yesterday that the first thirty-six Klapperschlanges would be ready for transport at the specified date. And that is still true."

"Don't take that tone with me," Buckler said ominously.

"Sorry, major. We are all under great strain. Protect the factory, and we will deliver as promised."

Krafft was right about the strain, and he had been clever enough to turn the problem back to Buckler.

"Can't you urge them to speed up the work?" he urged.

"They are working twenty-four hours a day already, major."

Buckler tried another tack. "It will be your neck, too, if the enemy finds a way to destroy that factory. You are in the midst of a high priority target."

Krafft spoke as if he were addressing a persistent child. "You know what our rocket can do. We can batter the enemy as well as you can."

If Hauptmann Krafft knew how bankrupt the fighter defenses were, he would never have made that last idiotic statement, Buckler thought. He hung up the receiver in irritation and walked through the monastery's great hall, his heels clacking on the stone flooring.

The sun flooded over him as he swung open the tall front doors, but he shuddered in its heat. Fighter weather.

Behind him, the telephone shrilled and he heard a noncom answer. Then the man was at his side.

"Telephone report, sir. Thirty P-51's coming in from due west."

"How many minutes?"

"Fifteen, sir."

Barely time to reach his own plane, in a pasture four miles distant, and get in the air. He dashed toward his nearby staff car as Stoltzman appeared, as if by magic, from another door in the building and ran for the driver's side. The gears clashed, and they lurched along country lanes, skidding wildly on the sharp turns and bouncing high across ruts in the dirt roadway.

At least our radio network operates properly, Buckler noted with satisfaction as Stoltzman pulled the car beside his plane beneath the concealing trees. The engine was idling smoothly, and the two mechanics assigned to his FW signaled that it was fully fueled and armed.

He vaulted into the cockpit, buckling his parachute leg straps as one of the mechanics adjusted straps over his

132

shoulders. The chocks were pulled free, and he rammed the throttle home, rolling the cockpit canopy shut as the fighter leaped forward.

The leggy landing gear jounced across the uneven pasture. Then the field fell away and he was in the air, grabbing for altitude, his radio crackling reports from ground control.

"Enemy fighters now four minutes west of Rtanj, according to the ground observer in that area. Altitudes less than one thousand meters. Second group of unidentified fighters now reported by radar twenty kilometers northwest at fifteen thousand meters. Due east heading. Will pass twenty kilometers north this area."

That was strange. First comes a report of one group at low level, heading straight for his sector. Then radar finds a second group high and obviously a good distance away. That would be a diversion flight, of course. Now he knew what had happened. The low group hadn't expected to be spotted until they were almost on top of him. But they didn't know about the spotters he had stationed at long intervals all the way to the coast. They had eyes and telephones, and they had revealed the enemy's strategy.

"Assemble on me," Buckler ordered. The scattered Focke-Wulfs rising from a dozen separate fields closed in and followed him southward beyond Rtanj Mountain.

"Enemy now making ground attack," the controller announced. Buckler immediately swung his group around the western skirt of Rtanj and burst upon the scene in a long dive. They caught the strafing P-51's flat-footed. Two of them never came out of their runs across the all-but-deserted airfield. They simply wobbled and plunged into the woods beyond the monastery.

The rest of the Mustangs scattered and began to work the

133

dogfight westward. Buckler realized what they were up to, and he wasn't going to buy it. The attack force was now trying to become the diversion. No doubt they had already radioed the other group to the north to swing around behind his squadron. Buckler had been chewed up between two Mustang groups before, and he wasn't about to give it another try.

"Break off," he ordered. The Americans were at the limit of their range and had used a lot of ammunition. They had to head home, and they did. The Focke-Wulfs whirled, free, sniffing for new prey.

"Fighters attacking the valley." The controller's voice was a degree higher-pitched than usual.

The valley? There could be only one valley worth attacking, Buckler realized. They were after The Project. But what could fighters accomplish with their little fragmentation bombs against the huge concrete door of the factory?

Not until his slim fighter burst over the valley did Buckler discover that he was at the mercy of American strategy once again. A greasy ball of blue-gray smoke rolled up the face of the underground factory. The floor of the valley was a cauldron of crimson flame.

He hadn't seen it before, but he knew what it was. Napalm. They were trying to warp the tracks. A lot of good that would do. By tomorrow, the repair crews would have new tracks laid, and no time would have been lost at all.

The ground controller came in loud and rasping. "Bombers on radar. Small flight, thirty thousand kilometers high, just south of Rtanj Mountain."

That miserable mountain. The winds around it never changed direction, and that had let the German engineers lay out an airfield with a single runway. But they couldn't get heavy radio units to its craggy tip, and the massive mountain blocked radar to the south. The enemy was again using this weakness to its full advantage.

The Mustangs had finished dumping their napalm into the seething valley, and now they were all over Kommando Boelcke like wasps from a broken nest.

Buckler dropped away from a stream of tracers reaching for his left wing tip. Trees rushed at him, and he yanked the nose level, trying to squeeze out of the battle from the bottom.

He was entirely willing to stay and fight; eager to do so, in fact. But he had learned much in the past weeks. If the Americans were sending in three bombers above this elaborate two-pronged diversion, then those bombers carried something that must be destroyed. He had to get them. Again he ordered Pichler's group to follow.

"I am only seven," Pichler replied.

"That will have to do," Buckler said. He felt that eight planes could leave the widespread dogfight and streak south at treetop level without pulling a pack of Mustangs with them.

It almost worked. But as the eight Focke-Wulfs leaped from their ground level southward lunge and howled steeply upward, a half-dozen P-51's broke off their individual duels and roared in pursuit.

"They've spotted us." The voice on the B-24 intercom belonged to Stav Kavalla, and it made Skinny's gloved fingers tighten on the knobs of the bomb sight. He leaned forward and peered through the plastic nose housing. There they were, seven FW's, tiny and bright against the dark mountains. He couldn't afford to worry about them for the moment. The bomb release point was only seconds away.

Skinny adjusted the sight, and the B-24 responded. Its controls were locked into the sighting device during the bomb run. The end of the valley moved downward in the sight screen toward the bomb release cross hair. A fat smoke smudge marked the napalm attack. Skinny's thumb rested on the release button. The target reached the cross hair and he punched the button.

"First bomb away."

The corrugated bomb bay doors rolled shut, and control went back to Jesse in the pilot's seat. A thousand feet below, the Azon's flare ignited bright white.

At that moment, Marty Fields' B-24, riding five hundred feet behind Jesse's, released its first Azon. As its tail flare bloomed brilliant red, the third B-24 in the line of three dropped its missile. A few seconds later Joe Carrone's Azon burned a lime-green tail light. The radio-controlled bombs dwindled into a chain of three glowing lights, streaking across the rugged Yugoslavian hills.

As the third light flamed into life below him, Jesse reduced power. Fields climbed into position above and slightly behind his left wing. On his right, Joe Carrone pulled into a lower defense position. Jesse was glad to see them there because this was going to be a long and tough grind.

His fingers deftly adjusting the azimuth control toggle, Skinny followed the descending trio of lights. He swung his Azon sharply left. The red and green coded Azons guided by the bombagators in Fields' and Carrone's Liberators veered to follow his.

"Fifteen seconds to impact." Skinny turned the Azon another three degrees as he made the announcement.

"Seven bogies closing in at ten o'clock low," Jesse warned.

The white-tailed Azon sailed into the valley in a long curve, slammed against the solid rock east wall short of the target and disappeared in the napalm smoke.

"Near miss," Skinny said, "but the three-second delay could have helped with a ricochet."

Smoke and rock fragments spurted upward above the valley rim as the Azon detonated. On the heels of the first blast, Fields' red-tailed Azon crashed into the valley—a quarter-mile short. The shock wave uprooted scrubby bushes on both slopes. The third Azon plunged between the first two and threw a gray smoke ring rolling high above the slopes.

"Two misses and a maybe," Skinny said grimly, "but it's a sure bet that they won't be launching any of their rockets at us today."

"They won't have to," Hunky Molnar blurted. "Here come the local firemen."

"We've got work to do," Jesse said tensely. He banked the lumbering bomber to the right, and the two flanking B-24's followed as if they'd been glued there.

A kilometer distant, Erwin Buckler still couldn't believe it. Three unescorted B-24's were like a gift. He twisted his head around the armor plate behind him. Had he actually seen what he thought he had! The stick came back, and he stood the FW on its nose then hauled it over on its back and snap-rolled to recover heading back across the bomber flight.

Yes, it was true, unbelievably true. The lead ship wore the number 401 on its twin rudders!

"Pichler," he almost shouted. "The middle bomber is mine. You understand?"

"*Ja*," the squadron leader answered. "But it should not be difficult. It has no turrets."

Pichler was correct. That was strange indeed. Buckler drew closer, straining forward with curiosity. A sky full of tracers leaped at him and he broke away once more. Number 401 had no turrets, but his friends made up for it. He'd never seen such firing from just two bombers.

And now more tracers came from behind him. The Mustangs had reached the scene.

Hauptmann Ludwig Krafft, twenty-thousand meters below the aerial battle, had felt the cold fingers of fear when the Mustangs howled up the valley. It was the first fighter attack on the factory, and he was sure the enemy knew fighters could not even dent the heavy entrance door. That was what worried him. What surprises did they have up their sleeves this time?

The door, usually left open at least four meters for vehicular access, clanked shut barely ten seconds before the first Mustang twisted down the winding canyon and screeched across the face of the cliff that housed the underground installation.

"Fire bombs!" the observation bunker telephoned an instant later. "The valley is burning right up to the door."

Trying to warp the tracks, Krafft correctly guessed. Well, that was a night's work to repair.

Less than three minutes later, the bunker atop the cliff called again. "Three bombers. High to the south." A pause, then, "We can see the bombs. Three of them. They are too far to the right. They will miss. They——" The high-pitched words stopped with a gasp.

"Was ist los?" Krafft shouted. "What's the matter up there?"

"The bombs," the observer managed to get out. "They turned in mid-air. They are going to——"

His words were drowned in the tremendous detonation that shook the solid floor of the cavern. Seconds later another explosion rattled the two dozen rockets assembled on

138

their flat cars in the factory's main chamber. A third blast sent another chain of tremors through the factory.

Krafft leaped into the elevator and streaked to the top of the mountain, emerging into a bunker of white-faced observers. "Pay attention to your work!" he shouted at the four severely shaken men. "Forget yourselves. The safety of the factory is the importance here."

He seized a pair of field glasses and leaned into the forward observation slot. The three bombers had swung south and were apparently lining up for another run. "What was that business about steerable bombs?" he asked without taking his eyes off the B-24's. The Focke-Wulfs had just reached them, and he heard the faint riveting sounds of aerial machine-gun fire.

"All three bombs turned in flight, sir. The first glanced off the far side of the valley and must have exploded against the door. We couldn't see because of the smoke. The other two hit further down the valley."

The three bombers were turning northward again. Krafft swung open the door of the bunker and stepped into the sunlight. In the valley below him, the smoke had lifted. He peered over the edge of the cliff and his heart seemed to turn over. Far below, a jagged crack ran across the face of the giant factory door. The first heavy bomb had ricocheted off the valley side, then bounced from the hard canyon floor straight into the door.

"Hauptmann! They have dropped three more. You must get back in the bunker."

He raised the field glasses. Three tiny dots hung in the sky below the bombers. What was the rule? If bombs seem to be climbing, they will strike behind you. If they are dropping, they will fall short. But if they simply hang in the sky, growing larger, then you are the target.

139

He scurried back to the bunker and the door clanged shut behind him. Through the observation slot, he watched, horrified, as the bombs made lurching corrections in their trajectories.

"Incredible!" he murmured. He grabbed the telephone and gambled his military career on a sudden decision.

"Evacuate the factory through the rear-escape tunnels," he barked. "Immediately. Do not quibble. You have only minutes left."

Beneath him, he knew the alarm klaxons were echoing along the cavern's corridors. Hundreds of scientists, manufacturing personnel, and security people pressed far back into the cavern to the steep emergency exits that would bring them to the surface in the scattered woods nearly a kilometer from the factory entrance.

Now that he had made the decision, Krafft found his hands shaking uncontrollably, but not from the terror of the approaching bombs that eerily changed course as they fell. What had planted a lump of ice in his stomach was the knowledge that he had just completely halted high-priority production, and if the factory survived, he would not.

The first bomb struck the face of the cliff not two hundred meters from the bunker. They braced themselves for the explosion, but it came a long moment later and from far below the cliff's edge.

"Time fuse," Krafft guessed. "The bomb fell to the bottom before it went off."

The second missile soared over their heads and clumped into the open area three hundred meters beyond. Its blast, three seconds after impact, peppered the bunker with a shower of stone fragments.

The third bomb sailed into the valley in a looping curve

and dropped below the rim of the hill. The detonation was muffled, but Krafft felt its power when the entire bunker seemed to leap a full inch upward.

The three bombers had begun another wide swing southward. "And now we ourselves must go," Krafft ordered. He opened the bunker door and motioned his three men outside. They stood blinking in the sunshine. Above them, the air battle had spread over miles of open sky. Vapor trails sketched a random network of white yarn across the blue-white backdrop. The howls of straining engines and the distant popping of machine guns held the bunker men in motionless fascination.

"You think the bombers will wait until you find cover?" Krafft shouted. "Move!" He set out across the rocky ground in a rubber-legged trot toward the woods a half-mile north, and his men followed uncertainly, staring back over their shoulders at a descending black plume that marked the fall of a stricken fighter plane. Far to the south, the three B-24's banked steeply into their final run.

FOURTEEN

Not a man aboard the Liberators had been sure he could take repeated bomb runs and still do his job as it was supposed to be done. Yet, as they once again drummed north, the three crews found tremendous pride in how tightly their little formation had hung together, how well they had managed to disrupt the Focke-Wulf runs, and in the fact that they had apparently made two hits squarely on the target.

Jesse's plane was already hard pressed. The left wing had been chewed by cannon fire, and in the bomber's wake streamed a thin, ominous streak of black oil. On the second bomb run, Pastore and Carrone's regular ball turret man had combined their four guns to stagger a Focke-Wulf in a mid-climb. But just before he fell away, the pilot opened up with everything he had, and a shell thudded into 401's number four engine, severing an oil line.

The Mustangs were alert and well coordinated, racing in

to cut off the FWs the instant they broke out of the fighter battle to attack the bombers. There was one Focke-Wulf pilot, though, who was unbelievably good. He managed to snake past the protective Mustang screen without showing a single hit. Time after time, he barreled across the three B-24's, chipping away with his infernal cannon.

Jesse checked his engine instruments and punched the mike button. "Skinny, we're losing oil on number four. I don't know if she'll take two more runs."

"I'm going to drop the last two Azons together, anyway, Jess. They're both on the same frequency. I can guide them both at once."

"Getting pretty confident, aren't you?"

"You bet I am. You see that last one? Right in the barn. These next two are going to do it."

The bomb bay doors rolled open for the last time. Fields and Carrone pulled in close, their gunners' faces visible in the turrets. The other two B-24's were flying gun platforms, now that their Azons were gone, and their only duty now was to protect Jesse's plane.

The familiar valley drifted into the bomb sight's screen. Skinny knew the exact aiming point now. He waited one more split second and punched the release button twice. "Both bombs away," he sang out. "Let's go home."

The three Liberators wheeled northwestward as the flare lights broke out below them and streaked for the valley. Skinny let the two Azons drift eastward, wide of the target; then he kicked in full left turn control. The twin lights swung in a lazy arc, skimmed the mountain crags, streaked straight for the upper end of the valley.

At the last instant, Skinny toggled a sharp right turn, leading the reaction delay precisely. The twin lights winked out at the base of the target. For long seconds, nothing.

143

Then a yellow flash kicked a huge burst of smoke down the valley. The mountain seemed to tremble. A gush of orange leaped from the mouth of the underground factory, and huge sections of the entrance door flew into the air.

"We got a secondary explosion!" Skinny yelled. "We busted through!"

The base of the mountain was racked by blast after blast as the fuel and warhead storage areas blew up. A huge mushroom of smoke rolled above the valley, and at its base, the factory tore itself to rubble.

Jesse's crew went wild on the intercom but he didn't bother to quiet them down. He completed his due west swing, hunched into his flak vest and poured the coal to all four engines. This was the homeward leg. Nothing could happen now.

The fighter attacks had broken off sharply. Out of ammo, he guessed. By the time they landed and rearmed, the B-24's would be long gone. It worked two ways, though. "Big Friends, Big Friends," the Mustang group commander radioed suddenly. "Got to leave you."

"Roger, Little Friends. Thanks and luck." The Mustangs had run low on ammo, too. And no doubt their fuel gauges were sending out danger signals. They veered northwest toward their own base, and the sky was clear. Almost.

"One bogie at seven o'clock high," Terrible Cochran reported. "It's that same persistent character. Why doesn't he go home? There's nothing left down there for him to defend."

The German fighter raced in high, just out of range. Directly above the bomber formation, it rolled on its back, the nose dropped, and it arrowed straight down. Tracers leaped upward from the bombers flanking Jesse. Orange flashed along the fighter's wings. The first handful of cannon shells

144

chipped off 401's left wing tip. A second burst hit the left outboard engine. The propeller flopped around uselessly.

"Feather number one," Jesse rapped. Stav hit the button.

Jesse had his hands full. A dead engine and a damaged aileron on the same side were bad business. The left wing dropped. He pulled it back up with sheer muscle, but it dropped again.

Marty Fields' voice came over the command set. "Hang on. We'll stick with you."

"No," Jesse ordered. "You hold your heading. We'll make it on our own." Fields and Carrone had a total of twenty-two men aboard. Jesse wasn't about to let twenty-two men and two planes try to save one plane with a skeleton crew of five.

He sank out of formation, one engine dead and another not far from it. Above him, the other two B-24's pushed westward, huddling together in the lonely sky. There were good men up there, some of them his own, and Jesse knew how they felt about his order to stay on course and leave him to the wolves.

He smiled bitterly at the unintentional pun. Actually, there was just one Wulf—but that was going to be enough. The German fighter swung into a long, skidding pursuit curve, carefully staying out of range of both the nose and tail gun. A package of cannon shells whistled into the right wing. Number three engine stopped cold.

"Feather it," Jesse said.

Stav's face was white above his oxygen mask. "Can't. Hydraulic line's gone."

The B-24 wallowed below ten thousand feet, and the oxygen masks came off. Jesse forced his voice into a flat calmness on the interphone.

"We're going down with two engines out and aileron

control partly shot away. I'll give you each a choice. You can bail out or stick with me for a landing. She's a light ship without turrets and I think I can hold her. No guarantees, though. Any guy wants to use a chute might be a lot smarter than me. How about it, Terrible?"

From the tail, Terrible Cochran's voice sounded thin and distant. "I'll stick."

"So will I," Hunky Molnar boomed from the flight deck.

"You need all the help you can get," Stav put in. "I'll hang around to see whether or not you're really a good pilot."

Skinny came on the intercom with a snort. "You don't think I'm going to be the only guy to test fly a parachute!"

"Then get up here," Jesse ordered. "If the whole hydraulic system is shot out, we won't be able to get the wheels down and that nose will cave in like paper. Terrible and Hunky, I want you up here, too. With the top turret gone, the flight deck should be the safest spot. Where's that fighter, somebody?"

"Circling," Hunky reported from the left waist. "He knows he's got us."

"Where you going to put us down?" Stav asked, scanning the scattered fields five thousand feet below them.

"At the nearest airport."

"You mean that fighter field?"

"Got any better ideas?" Jesse swung around in his seat and peered back at the flight deck. Hunky and Skinny were climbing up from the lower crawlway. "Cochran, where are you?"

"I want to get a final shot at that guy."

"No! Absolutely not. He's been playing with us for some reason. He could have blown us out of the air easily. Let him alone and get up here."

146

The Liberator faltered below three thousand. Jesse banked cautiously around the mountain south of the fighter field.

"I want everyone in crash position right now."

The three men on the flight deck lay on their backs, heads cradled in their hands and feet forward against the bulkhead behind the pilot's compartment.

The bomber swept around the eastern skirt of Rtanj Mountain and the fighter field drifted into view. Jesse and Stav, straining together, brought the left wing up with full wheel and hard right rudder.

"Wheels down."

Stav hit the lever. "Nothing, Jess."

"Try manual."

"Still nothing."

"How about flaps?"

"No good, either."

"This is going to be one sweet landing, isn't it?"

"You bet your babushka."

Jesse flashed his co-pilot an appreciative grin. Stav had nerve enough for all of them.

The scrubby bushes at the end of the runway flowed toward them and flashed by at more than a hundred miles an hour. The bright green sod runway raced beneath the nose. Jesse eased back the flabby control wheel. The tail settled, feeling for the ground.

"Cut 'em, Stav."

The two good engines died, and the bomber was filled with an eerie screech of rushing air. The tail hit, and the B-24 bellied in heavily. The nose greenhouse exploded in a thousand particles of plastic that rattled back over the fuselage like hail.

The jar threw Jesse against his seat belt. The right wing

digging a huge furrow in the turf, the bomber slewed around to the left, throwing the three crewmen on the flight deck against the right wall in a tangle of arms and legs.

Dirt fountained over the cockpit windows as the nose dug in deeply. The tail lifted high, then fell back with a crash.

Silence. Then Jesse unbuckled his seat belt with a flat, "Who's hurt?"

"I guess a bloody nose isn't much of a fee for being alive," Skinny gasped, exploring the rest of his face with cautious finger tips.

"All right, let's get out of here. There's still plenty of gas aboard this bus."

Skinny tore the flare gun out of its flight deck bracket as he scrambled through the top hatch just behind the pilot's seats.

"You gonna signal for help?" asked Hunky Molnar.

"Move!" Jesse urged from below. He boosted them out frantically, then heaved himself through the opening. "Come on, Skinny. Get it over with."

The bombagator aimed the flare pistol at a growing puddle of gasoline beneath the shattered wing and fired. The red flare sizzled into the gas, and flame ran along the grass under the crumpled bomber. The wreckage caught with a dull whoosh. "That takes care of the bombsight and the Azon guidance system," Skinny said with satisfaction. "Now what?"

"It's not up to us," said Jesse. "Look."

A little group of German soldiers was running toward them, rifles ready.

"I thought this place would be crawling with Germans," Hunky said. "Is that the best they can do?"

148

Behind them, the furiously burning B-24 threw a black column high into the noon sky.

"Doesn't matter how many of them there are," Jesse said. "We aren't going any place."

FIFTEEN

It had been too much to hope for, but nevertheless at this very minute the pilot of B-24 Number 401 was on his way with his crew to Buckler's monastery headquarters. There had been only five on the crew when the bomber crash-landed, Buckler had been told. He had landed back at his pasture strip after he had seen the B-24 crash at the all-but-abandoned main fighter base. That had been strange, the urge of his not to face the pilot of 401 until he had had time to prepare himself.

He had radioed urgent instructions to hold the crew for his personal interrogation, and now, not two hours after they had been shot down, they were en route to the monastery.

He would receive them not in his miserable little office, but in the huge dining hall, and he had ordered all the mess orderlies to clear out. Now he paced nervously among the deserted tables. This was the moment he had lived for, and he was going to savor it to the fullest. He wished he could be alone with the pilot, but that was impossible because he knew no English. Stoltzman must interpret.

Buckler glanced nervously at his wrist chronometer. Why was it taking so long? He drew a cup of coffee from the urn at the end of the serving counter, carefully dumped in a level teaspoonful of brownish sugar, then left the coffee untouched.

He sat stiffly on one of the mess benches and drummed his fingers on the table. Where were they? Where?

The dining hall door partially opened and Stoltzman slid in. "Where do you want them, major?"

"In he——" He cleared his dry throat. "In here," he said again.

The five prisoners filed in, followed by two Wehrmacht soldiers with machine pistols drawn. "You two wait outside," Buckler ordered, and the soldiers withdrew, closing the door behind them.

The prisoners were an oddly-assorted lot, dressed in rumpled khaki flying suits and, of course, hatless. They stood at a sort of loose attention, far from cowed, but not defiant, either, as they gazed about the dining hall.

Buckler's eyes ranged down the row. A squat dark man, a big boyish-looking one, a green-eyed wiry one: those were the officers. And only two enlisted men? A careless boy with a loose mop of hair, and a square-jawed muscular middle-European type.

"Where is your pilot?" he said crisply. "Translate, Stoltzman."

His fox-faced orderly labored through the English version, but the prisoners weren't listening. Their eyes had found Buckler's sad excuse for a face, and he slapped his

151

hand against the table. "Wait, Stoltzman. Tell them it was a fire that cost me my face. Then tell them I want to know what happened to their pilot." Stafford, the sly little Cockney he envisioned, had obviously somehow managed to escape.

Stoltzman was telling them about the face—Buckler caught the word *fire,* much like the German *Feuer*—and they seemed to understand. In fact, if he let his imagination run away with him, he could almost fancy that he saw a certain degree of sympathy in their faces.

But these were only the crewmen. He wanted the pilot. "Stoltzman!" he barked. "Find out where the pilot is."

Stoltzman turned and went to work. The big boy-like man stepped forward and jabbed his own chest with his thumb.

"He says he is the pilot, major."

"He has replaced Stafford?"

The enemy crew seemed to stiffen when he said, "Stafford."

"He says he *is* Stafford."

"But Stafford isn't like that! He——" Buckler stopped and Stoltzman stared at him.

"Sir?"

"Nothing." His head was whirling. It was incredible. This boy couldn't possibly be the enemy who had caused him to fight so hard for life in a Berlin hospital; who had made him survive from day to day for this sweet moment of revenge.

"Ask him——" Buckler's voice trembled but he caught it in time. "Ask him if he remembers shooting down a fighter plane about . . . about eight months ago. He pretended to surrender, then he shot the plane down."

Stoltzman's translation was endless. The big pilot made him stop once, put in a comment, then listened closely. When Stoltzman finished, the American offered a few

152

clipped sentences, his face showing a mixture of emotions.

"He says it was only five months ago," Stoltzman relayed.

Buckler was jolted. Only five months . . .

"He says he had a badly wounded man aboard and an engine inoperative. The fighter pilot, he says, was playing with them, and that made him angry. Because of the wounded man, he did what he did. He also says, major, that the rest of his crew is blameless. They did only what he ordered."

Buckler stepped close to Stafford. There was no arrogance in the American's green-brown eyes. Nor fear, either. Buckler considered his next question carefully, unconsciously running the tip of his tongue along his numb upper lip.

"Ask him, Stoltzman," he said at last, "ask him if he is proud of that day."

Again the agony of translation and retranslation. Stoltzman turned to Buckler. He had clearly gathered that a lot more was going on here than a simple interrogation.

He watched Buckler's eyes closely. "The American says *Nein,* Herr Major. He is not proud of what he did."

"Do you believe him?" If Stoltzman thought Stafford was telling the truth, then all Buckler had been living for was in danger of being undermined.

The aide shrugged. *"Ja,* I think he tells the truth. Why would he lie?"

The tenseness that had held him with such urgency for almost half a year seemed to drain into the stone floor, and Buckler said vacantly, "Ask him where the rest of his crew is." He really didn't care. He didn't hate this man he was supposed to hate, and that was beyond understanding. The dual-language discussion merged into a distant garble.

153

"Herr Major," Stoltzman said, puzzled at Buckler's inattention. "Sir?"

"What is it?"

"He says his name is Jesse C. Stafford. His rank is First Lieutenant. His serial number is——"

"Why did he speak so willingly of the other business, then?"

The translation. The answer. Stoltzman turned. "That was a personal matter, the pilot says. He wanted to set the record straight. But that is all he will say, and now it is to be name, rank, and serial number."

"That ends it, I think." Buckler was no interrogation officer, and what did it matter anyway? The factory was no more. The Americans looked tired, and he was tired, too.

"One more thing, major," Stoltzman said. He could certainly be irksome at times. He handed Buckler a form. "You have had the prisoners consigned to you, and you must designate their camp."

"I thought that was up to the unit in Belgrade."

"Not in this case. They don't want to transship. The prisoners will leave directly from here."

Buckler studied the form. He had a choice. He gazed at Stafford thoughtfully; tapped his pen against his teeth. Then he made a deliberate check mark, glared at Stoltzman, and signed the form. Now he, too, could live with himself. His eyes found Stafford's and he clicked his heels together in a little bow from the waist. Surprisingly, the American saluted. Not the captured acknowledging the captor; but one airman saluting another.

Buckler strode into the hall. "See that they eat, Stoltzman."

The lean-faced aide squinted at the form. His eyes widened. He called the two guards, motioned toward the

154

dining room's serving area, then scurried through the great hall after Buckler.

"Herr Major, you have made an error. Perhaps you are unfamiliar with the form. You should have indicated a German prison camp, a homeland camp. But you have checked a camp near Sofia. You know that Rumania will be taken by the Russians in a few weeks. The Americans will be liberated before the month is out." He stopped. His commander was pointedly ignoring him.

Buckler had folded his arms, and he leaned against the doorway of the old monastery, gazing high into the flawless sky.

"Have you noticed, Stoltzman, what a beautiful day it is? Even the hills seem alive. Why is it I've never seen the beauty of this place before?"

Stoltzman looked at him for a long moment. For the first time since Buckler's return from Berlin, the major seemed to look more like his old self.

The mood was catching. "You are quite correct, sir," Stoltzman said in a surprisingly soft voice. "It is indeed a fine afternoon."

REFERENCES

Bombs Away! New York: William H. Wise & Co., Inc., 1947.

CECIL STEWARD. *Serbian Legacy.* New York: Harcourt, Brace & Co., 1959.

EDMUND STILLMAN AND THE EDITORS OF LIFE. *The Balkans.* New York: Time, Inc., 1964.

J. R. SMITY. *The Focke-Wulf FW190D/Tal52.* Leatherhead, Surrey: Profile Publications, Ltd., 1966.

ROGER A. FREEMAN. *The Consolidated B-24J Liberator.* Leatherhead, Surrey: Profile Publications, Ltd., 1965.

Consolidated B-24. New York: Air Age Technical Library, Air Age, Inc., 1944.

MARTIN C. WINDROW. *The Messerschmitt Bf 109E.* Leatherhead, Surrey: Profile Publications, Ltd., 1965.

EIICHIRO SEKIGAWA. *German Military Aircraft in the Second World War.* Tokyo: Kantosha Co., Ltd., 1959.

Target: Germany. New York: Simon and Schuster, 1943.

History of the 456th Bomb Group (H). Cerignola, Italy: Public Relations Section, 456th Bomb Group, 1945.

WILLIAM F. HALLSTEAD

A native of Dalton, Pennsylvania, William F. Hallstead has been writing for nearly twenty years. He has written well over 200 stories and articles—which have appeared in such magazines as *Popular Science, Motor Trend, Woman's Day, Boy's Life, Mechanix Illustrated, Scholastic Teacher,* and *Flying*—and several books, of which the most widely known is *Dirigible Scout,* published in 1967. He has also contributed to more than a dozen high school English textbooks and anthologies.

Mr. Hallstead graduated from The Hill School in Pottstown, Pennsylvania, in time to enlist in the Army Air Force in 1942. He taught both Morse Code and radio navigation, but finally was assigned to a heavy bomber crew in 1945. Because of mechanical troubles enroute to the European combat zone, however, Hallstead's plane limped into its base in Italy only in time to fly one mission before the war was over. His aviation experience continued with post-war jobs in crop-dusting, an attempt to found a glider pilot school, work as a flight instructor, and teaching ground school.

In 1952, Mr. Hallstead was commissioned to write the 31st Hardy Boys book, *The Secret of Wildcat Swamp.* Because the book appeared under the name of the original writer of the series, it was, in Mr. Hallstead's words, "great for the bank account, but hard on the ego." In 1961, he put together some of his short stories, some of which had previously appeared in magazines, under the title of *Ev Kris, Aviation Detective. Dirigible Scout,* published more recently, was based in part on a boyhood visit to Lakehurst, New Jersey, to see the old Hindenburg. His latest work, *The Missiles of Zajecar,* draws heavily on the author's background of service on B-24 Liberators and an interest in rockets. *Sky Carnival,* his fifth book, will be published in the late spring of 1969.

Mr. Hallstead, his wife Jean, and their two children live in Lutherville, Maryland, a suburb north of Baltimore. At present, while continuing his free-lance writing, Mr. Hallstead is Director of Publications for the Maryland Center for Public Broadcasting.